BITTEN WITCH

SILVER WOLVES OF LOCKWOOD

BOOK ONE

WHITNEY MORSILLO

If you purchased this book without a cover, you should be aware that this book is stolen property. It was reported as "unsold and destroyed," and the author has not received any payment for this "stripped book."

This book is a work of fiction. The names, characters, businesses, places, events, locales, and incidents are the products of the author's imagination or have been used fictitiously and are not to be construed as real. Any resemblance to actual persons, living or dead, actual events, locales or organizations is entirely coincidental.

ISBN 9798394147685

Copyright © 2023 by Whitney Morsillo.

All rights reserved. Published independently by Whitney Morsillo, and any associated logos are trademarks and/or registered trademarks of Whitney Morsillo.

To all the abuse victims of a parent, a partner, anyone: you are stronger than you're allowed to believe, and "the sooner you realize that you have every right to fight back, the more powerful you'll become."

She was his light;
He was her darkness.
The stars whispered among them,
The troubles,
The rumors,
The pain.
But none knew that his darkness caressed hers at night.
None knew that her light lit him up from inside,
That he wrapped her so tightly in his arms
The arrows never pierced her,
Or that she didn't smooth his jagged edges
But fit her own tight against them.
The only thing that was spoken,
The truth no one dared question,
Was that to lay a finger on one
Meant to seek the wrath of the other.
For the others who had touched her
Had their screams added to the chorus of Tartarus,
I didn't know, I didn't know,
I didn't know.
But they did.
They just wished he didn't.

CHAPTER ONE
Adara

THE LEAVES CRUNCH UNDER MY BOOTS, A TRAIL of fiery orange, blood red, and golden yellow swirling on the dirt path around me. A million stars dust the clear, inky sky, shining through the branches as they shed their foliage. Sighing, I bring my head back down to my boots, mutilating the beautiful leaves on the ground in front of me. I don't deserve such beauty—not the stars, not even these leaves. If I could walk with my eyes closed, I would, because that's what I deserve—darkness—for being a traitor to my coven… even if it's for a reason born of love. It's why I left after the sun had gone down, just enough silvery light of the moon guiding my way. Though, I'm grateful it's the night before the full moon.

Tripping over a root arching up from the ground, I stumble and scrape my palm on the rough bark of the oak that caught me. "Damn it," I hiss, the sharp stinging in my palm stealing my focus for a moment and making me forget where I am. My gaze snaps up, darting back and forth between the trees as my mouth goes dry. I need to be more careful, this is the Silver Wolf Pack territory. Licking my lips, I curl my fingers into my palm and bring it to my chest, then continue on the hidden path before me.

Silver Lycans, the bar and gambling den on the other side of the forest that juts against the back edge of my mother's property, isn't far now. I can only hope that the pitiful amount of magic I have will conceal my scent for a few more hours while I'm among the wolves.

A warm breeze rustles the hair gathered at the nape of my neck, and I shiver—it's much too warm for a September night in New England. Swallowing hard, I keep my eyes trained on the ground before me and walk a bit faster, sweat gathering on my palms as I pull my jacket tighter around me. The sound of wings flapping grows closer, and my heart rate picks up, knowing any vile creature could be stalking me in this forest. A branch creaks as trees sway in the sudden breeze. Sharp claws cling onto my shoulder, startling me, and I whirl around with a barely contained scream.

Black feathers blend in with the night sky, and I clamp my eyes shut, trying to calm both my heart and my breathing.

"So, you were serious?"

Opening my eyes to glare at the raven, I watch as he simply tilts his head. "Kaylus, I swear to the gods, if you weren't my familiar, I would murder you on the spot."

He caws loudly, and I fight to not shove him off me. *"You'd be lost without me, and you know it."*

I scoff at his words as they sound in my mind, knowing they're true and unwilling to admit it. Kaylus has been my familiar for five years, since I turned fourteen, and he's been insufferable since—though making him live in the forest outside my house doesn't help his mood.

"I told you this was a bad idea. It was a bad idea the first night, and it's a bad idea now."

I stomp harder on the leaves before me, fighting to keep my voice low. "I *know* that, but what choice do I have? Jules deserves to go to the academy. I need the money for her tuition." Pressing my lips into a firm line, I scowl down at the forest floor as I walk. I was never invited to attend the Academy of Witches, but my sister is finally of age at fifteen and received her invitation to attend just last week.

"That's not your job, Addy. That's Monique's."

I swipe angrily at the tears running down my cheeks. "You know she won't, Kaylus. This is the only way."

Our mother refuses to let Jules explore her abilities—but my sister is exceptional. She's gifted and smart and *kind*. She deserves more than anyone to attend the academy and become who she's meant to be—the witch she's meant to be. But the day the invitation came was the day we suddenly became financially unable to afford anything beyond meager groceries and necessities. *"We just can't afford the tuition, sweetheart,"* Monique had said, but the words were hollow—lies.

It's how I ended up in this situation to begin with. Because the only way I can obtain money without my mother's knowledge is to gamble at Silver Lycans—and win.

"Cheating," Kaylus corrects, reading my thoughts. *"And he'll catch you eventually."*

"Gee, thanks," I mutter. Gritting my teeth, I try to push that fact—and the fear it brings—from my mind, but it's pointless. Gideon Disantollo, the owner of Silver Lycans and the alpha of the Silver Wolf Pack, is said to be the cruelest alpha in the country, if not in existence. He has a reputation for killing anyone attempting to steal from him—including cheating at cards—and he's so powerful that the wolf council has trouble controlling him. Fear curls in my gut, hard and cold like shards of ice, and I fight against the urge to turn around.

Jules needs this. She *deserves* this. I'll just have to be extra careful, that's all. I lift my chin, straightening my spine as my resolve strengthens, and continue my way through the forest. I'll only need to survive a few more nights anyway, then I'll have enough to cover the tuition for the academy—at least for the first year. After that, I can try to figure something else out—something less dangerous than a low magic witch entering lycan territory to cheat the most powerful alpha. Something that won't cost me my life if I'm caught—by Disantollo or Monique.

Sighing, I glance at the raven, but my words lodge in my throat as the bar comes into view just beyond the trees.

The low, flat building is painted black and would normally blend in with the shadows of the night if not for the neon white sign above the double doors depicting a howling wolf, its light reflecting off the glossy paint. I take a deep breath, anxiety rippling through me and fraying my nerves.

Kaylus takes off into the trees, settling himself on a branch to watch me cross through the tree line toward the entrance. *"This is a mistake, Addy."* His usually cocky voice holds a hint of concern, but I swallow back the rising panic and march through the edge of the forest to the bar.

Flinging the heavy metal door open, I quickly step inside, my senses assaulted by the loud music and musky air as I squint into the dim light. A long wooden bar runs the length of the room on the left side. The bartender appears more like a lumberjack than anything else. His thick auburn beard matches his slicked back shoulder length hair, and his buffalo plaid shirt is rolled to the elbows. He lifts his gaze from the glass he's drying, quirking one eyebrow as he takes me in. I lick my lips, hoping he doesn't recognize me from the last two nights.

A rock band plays on the small stage in the corner to my right, and the hardwood floor before it is cleared of tables to allow a space for dancing, which is littered with couples, all of their hands wandering enough to make my cheeks flush crimson. Turning, I make my way through the sea of people crowding around the bar. I weave through the round high-top tables, wrinkling my nose as I breathe in the heavy scent of beer and smoke that makes the air seem hazy and thick, until I reach the far wall in the back where there's a cluster of felt covered tables and card dealers.

Slinking down onto a bright red stool at one table in the back, I tuck a stray black strand of hair behind my ear and avoid making eye contact with the man beside me. His gut hangs over his belt, straining the buttons of his shirt, and a cigar dangles from his lips as he smirks at me, showing yellowed teeth.

"Ain't you a little young to be hangin' around here?" he asks, his voice slurring over the words as he pushes his greasy hair back from his face.

I cringe at his scrutiny, noting the near empty pint on the table in front of him before lifting my gaze to the dealer and holding out a wad of cash.

The dealer, who looks to be in his mid-forties—not that his age matters much when it comes to werewolves, stuck eternally at whatever age they are when they're turned—with a short trimmed black mustache and sharp green eyes, takes the cash from my hand and replaces it with three stacks of red chips. I place three chips in front of me, and the dealer sets one card, face up, in front of each person, then himself. I look down at my card—eight of hearts. As the next round is dealt, he sets down my second card—five of spades—before setting another card, face down, next to his own.

I keep my eyes on my cards while the rest of the table plays their hands, not wanting to appear as if I'm counting cards. I would, but I don't need to, thanks to the little bit of magic in my veins that for once doesn't have me feeling like the most helpless witch in the world. I might not be able to cast intricate spells like Jules or make healing potions like my grandmother, but this—small charms for hiding in plain sight—I can manage. Maybe it's because I've always felt invisible at home, and the moments when Monique does see me, I wish I *was* invisible just to escape her cruelty and her insults. Maybe it's because I've spent my life protecting Jules, helping her grow her powers whenever our mother wasn't home and training her so she might be noticed by the academy. And now I finally have a way to get the tuition money and make her dreams a reality. For once, I have use. I have power, small as my magic may be.

The dealer clears his throat, and I glance at the deck before looking at him—the top card glows a faint pink. "Hit me," I say, and the dealer flips a card face up in front of me without hesitating. A three of spades, but the deck still glows. "Hit me." Ace of hearts, and another pink glow. "Hit me."

My heart races, and my mouth goes dry. I'm already at seventeen, and the dealer's only face-up card is a jack of diamonds—ten points. If it's another ten, that gives him twenty...

The dealer sets down a four of clubs, and I fight to keep the smile from my face as I glance up at him. He raises his brows, then flips over his face down card—queen of diamonds.

The man beside me whistles, but I ignore him as I collect my winnings, then place another bet. I make sure I'm careful, not winning every round and never betting large amounts. As the hours pass, my confidence grows. It's been three nights, and I haven't been caught yet. I haven't even seen Disantollo in the bar—at least, I don't think I have, never having seen him before—and it only fuels my belief that I can do this. I need twenty-five thousand dollars to cover Jules's tuition for the first year, and after these last few nights, I have almost half of that so far.

I smile at the dealer and stand, knowing it's time to leave before I draw too much attention to myself. Plus, it's past midnight now, and I'll need to wake up in a few hours to make breakfast before Monique goes to work.

"One more hand, doll," the cigar man says.

I shake my head, fighting back the cringey feeling of his voice slithering over me, like spiders scuttling over my skin. "No, I really need to go."

He ignores me, looking at the dealer and waving his thick sausage fingers in the air at me. "She's in."

The dealer looks at me, waiting for me to answer, the rest of the table staring as well. I slowly lower back down onto my stool, not wanting to draw any more attention to myself. "Fine," I whisper, nodding at the dealer. I place five chips on the table, but the cigar man shakes his head.

"No, doll. You gotta match the table this round." He looks pointedly at me, and I swallow past the lump in my throat when I see his eyes glow silver—a trait of the Silver Wolf Pack.

I glance down the table, inwardly groaning when I see twenty chips stacked before each person before raising my five hundred dollar bet to two thousand. I wipe my damp palms on my thighs, glad the black leggings won't show the streaks of sweat, and gnaw on my inner cheek. I can't lose that kind of money, but I can't win without drawing all kinds of attention to myself, either.

The dealer sets a five of clubs in front of me, then a ten of spades in front of himself. On the next round, I get a king of spades. *Fifteen.* When it comes back to me again, I bounce my knee nervously, then force myself to sit still. *Don't show you're nervous. You have nothing to be nervous about. You're just here to play cards, just like everyone else.*

I swallow when I see the rosy glow coming from the deck, knowing I could win and be that much closer to getting the rest of the tuition money—eight freaking thousand dollars. Maybe the academy would take the rest later, during the second semester maybe, or as monthly payments. I lick my lips, steeling my nerves, and open my mouth. "Hit me," I whisper.

CHAPTER TWO
Gideon

STICKING TO THE SHADOWS OF MY LOW LIT BAR, I wander unseen to the dark wood bar top and lean against the wall. My gaze travels over the crowd, still dense despite the late hour. Couples dance and grind on the hardwood floor before the band, the heavy bass pulsing through the air. Tables littered throughout the space host people of varying levels of drunkenness, and the bar top is packed to the brim, everyone shouting their drink orders at Frank, fighting to be heard over the music even though they know he doesn't have to try hard to hear them. Wolves can hear impeccably well, after all.

  I let my eyes wander over the pool tables pushed against the wall, leaving the gambling green felt tables at the back wall for last. I grit my teeth against the hope swelling inside me. My body tenses when my gaze finally lands on the one person who caught my eye the moment she stepped inside. I inhale sharply through my nose, pressing my lips into a firm line when her sharp scent cuts through the musk of the bar. The first time I'd seen her, I thought she would smell light, floral. Like tulips after a rainstorm. But her deep, woodsy scent is earthy, yet feminine, like a wood nymph.

She tucks a wavy black strand of hair behind her ear, her posture stiff as she leans away from Wendell smoking his cigar next to her. I cross my arms over my chest, clenching my fists, when I notice the hunger in his eyes.

Lay one finger on her, and you'll only be able to hold that cigar in your right hand for the rest of your pathetic life, Wendell.

"She's here again," Frank's gruff voice cuts through my rage.

I grunt, glancing over at him before settling my stare back on the witch before me. "That's obvious."

He chuckles under his breath. "I figured you'd spot her first, but I didn't want to make assumptions, boss." Nodding briefly with a smirk, he ambles back behind the bar to fill another round of drinks for a curvy blonde who leans a little too far over the bar top, letting her low cut shirt expose more of her cleavage.

Despite the rush of people every night, Frank is the only bartender I employ. As my second in the pack, he's strong and fit, and the only one I trust to man the place when I'm not here. Even though he's friendly and flirts with almost anything that gives him the chance, he's able to keep tabs on every person in here without much effort and without letting anyone realize it—a skill I admire.

"Can I get you anything, handsome?" Aramin drawls, sliding next to me along the wall and tucking the waitress tray beneath her arm. She lingers a little too close, and her minty perfume burns in my throat.

I try to avoid her, knowing she's pouting when I don't acknowledge her fast enough, but she moves closer and angles herself into my line of vision, blocking the witch from view. "If I wanted something, I would've gotten it myself," I snap.

She huffs, tossing her fiery red hair over one shoulder. Her shirt is too tight and too low cut, making her chest swell with every breath, and I struggle to avoid rolling my eyes at her, acting like a petulant brat when she's been twenty for decades. "Fine, be like that then." She whirls around, sauntering over to her rowdiest table and plopping down into the lap of some guy who's drunk off his ass. I know she does it to bother me, to try to get under my skin for all the times I've rejected her, but I can't find it in myself to care. Three decades ago, I made the mistake of sleeping with her, and despite turning her down constantly since then, she hasn't backed down in the slightest.

Annoyed, I look back at the tables and see the young black haired woman start to stand, but Wendell stops her. "One more hand, doll," he says. I could carve his eyes out for that look in his eyes, and his tongue for that hideous pet name. She's no doll—especially not a *thing* of his. Though, I struggle to grasp why I care. Let Wendell have her, his wife will be sure to teach him a lesson, and her for coming here in the first place. But just the thought of him touching her—anyone touching her—makes blood pound in my ears.

She shakes her head, her voice determined but almost breathless, as if she didn't want to speak at all. "No, I really need to go."

Wendell waves his hand in her direction and talks to the dealer, Kurtis, and my eyes narrow into a glare.

She hesitates, glancing at Kurtis, then around the table, before slowly lowering herself back onto the stool. "Fine." It's a whisper, her irritation and discomfort evident, and I force myself to stay where I am, watching as she places her chips to bet.

"No, doll. You gotta match the table this round." My jaw clenches so hard, I'm worried my teeth will crack, and I barely register my fangs lengthening, until they pierce my bottom lip. Blood greets my tongue, and I take a deep breath through my nose, keeping my wolf at bay.

I shouldn't feel so damn protective over her. She's a witch—a cheating witch at that—who entered my bar when it's widely known her kind isn't welcomed within these walls, let alone within my pack territory. But for the last three nights, I've watched her and let her leave without a single consequence—and it's starting to feel like a weakness. One I can't allow to continue.

Wiping her hands on her pants, she matches the bet, stress marring her features. From here, I can only see her profile—the way she chews on the inside of her cheek, the small dimple that appears when she purses her lips to the side, the delicate curve of her jaw, the small slope of her nose. The lights are low, but over the last few nights, I've decided the darkness of her eyes are blue.

Kurtis hands out cards, one round, then two. Her hair sways slightly, the ends brushing against her lower back as she bounces her knee before suddenly stopping.

My brows furrow at her nervousness, noting she hasn't seemed outwardly anxious like this since she started coming here. Does she sense me? I glance around the bar, but no one has noticed my presence here. Not one but Frank, who smirks at me before returning to the overly friendly blonde from before, and Aramin, who is still purposefully ignoring me as she flirts with the customers. I suppress a growl and return my gaze to the back tables.

The girl is the last one in the row, and it's already her turn. She looks intensely at the deck, her tongue darting out to lick her lips. "Hit me," she whispers, her eyes glued to Kurtis's hand and the card he picks up.

Kurtis's eyes flick up, finding me immediately where I told him I'd be if she came back tonight and ran into trouble, as he moves to lay the card on the table. I push off the wall, drawing on my wolf to help me reach her side almost instantly. Her breath hitches when she sees the card—a perfect twenty-one—then she gasps when she catches sight of me, and I'm not foolish enough to think she knows who I am. I take a certain pleasure in staying hidden, not allowing photographs to be taken, and watching those who take my young, early twenties appearance as a surprise, squirming when I first strike.

My hand clamps around her wrist, wrenching her off the stool and bringing her to my side, and I narrow my eyes at Wendell, hunger swirling in his silver depths as he lowers the hand he'd raised to grab her with. "Hey, boss. I was just about to take care of this one for you." He draws on his cigar, smirking as he slowly rakes his gaze up and down the woman beside me.

I push against the rage threatening to rip my wolf to the surface so I can tear his throat out, not wanting to deal with the clean up of his blood from my walls. "I don't remember employing you in my guard, Wendell. How's the wife? It's awfully late. Past your curfew, isn't it?" I raise a brow at him, knowing if his wife caught wind of his wandering eye, he'd lose both and be blind—and divorced.

Wendell pales, the cigar hanging limply from his lips.

Satisfied, I tug the woman's wrist, pulling her along behind me. She barely comes up to my shoulder, and her forest perfume is invading my senses, making my wolf go wild. If I don't get her outside soon, where I can get a breath of fresh air into my lungs, I'm not sure what I'll do to her. Maybe I'll ravage her right in the middle of this bar—kick everyone out—or take her to my office until the sun rises.

Gritting my teeth, I shove open the door and yank her outside. The shock of the encounter is wearing off, and she stares at me with wide eyes—violet eyes. "So, they aren't blue," I say under my breath.

She wrenches her arm away, and I let her go, leaning back against the cold brick building and crossing my arms over my chest as I take her in for the first time up close. The white neon sign shines on her hair, reflecting like a raven's feather. Her eyes are like pools of amethyst—dark, purple, and ethereal—lined with thick black lashes. Her skin is pale, as if she's rarely been exposed to the sun, and her cheeks are flushed.

"I didn't gather my chips," she says, pressing her lips into a firm line.

My brows raise in surprise, not expecting her to stake a claim to her winnings when I can smell the fear wafting from her.

Her eyes narrow into slits. "That's it? You drag me out here without allowing me to collect my winnings and you have nothing to say?"

"Your winnings?" I ask quietly. "Are they still called that when you cheat, little witch?"

Her eyes widen, and her lips part as she sucks in a sharp breath. She stumbles back, and I shoot forward, my arm encircling her waist to keep her upright.

I lean down, my breath mingling with hers as I whisper, "You mask your scent well, but you should know better than to think you could fool me in my own territory."

She pushes against my chest, and I release her, stepping back to the brick wall. "Disantollo?" She breathes the single word harshly, like a curse.

But my name on her lips makes my wolf howl, and I struggle to force him down. "Hm. It seems you know my name, but I don't know yours."

"That's none of your business," she says, but her tone lacks the conviction of her words.

"Isn't it? Even when you're about to become a member of my pack?"

She takes a step back toward the tree line, away from the road, and her face loses the last bit of color it had. "I don't know what you're talking about."

A chuckle rumbles from my chest. "Darling, from the fear in your eyes, you know exactly what I'm talking about. No one cheats in my bar without consequences." Pushing off the wall, I reach her in two steps and whirl around, caging her against the building with my hands planted on the bricks by her head.

"B-but that's a death sentence," she whispers. "My coven will kill me..."

My lips graze her ear as I speak. "You should be thankful you get to leave here with your life and the money from the previous nights. Think twice before you cross me again. You won't be so lucky next time, little witch." I allow my wolf to come out, just enough to lengthen my fangs, as I bite down on her shoulder.

I know the minute her blood hits my tongue that it's a mistake. What should've been metallic and tangy, satisfying the bloodlust of my wolf, only tastes like a drink of water after walking the desert for months—gods damn lifesaving—and it only makes my wolf want her more.

She screams, her pain puncturing my heart like a blade, and I shove away from her, needing space between us as if she's a fire that's burned me. This can't be right. She's a witch for gods' sake! Damn it all to hell, there's no way...

A raven swoops down, clawing into her bloodied shoulder, breaking the spell of whatever nightmare was running through her mind—did she honestly think I would kill her? For some reason, the thought crushes my heart, making my chest ache. She rushes off into the woods, and I let her go, standing there wiping a hand across my mouth as if I could take it all back if I could get the taste of her blood out of my soul.

But there's no other explanation. I know it because I've tasted it before—once before, a lifetime ago. And it's a cruel twist of the Fates to give me another mate sentenced to die by the witches' hands.

Gods above, I just sentenced this woman, this witch—my one mate—to death by changing her into a werewolf. If the wolf's council doesn't come for her, her coven undoubtedly will, and right now, I can't decide which is worse—knowing her death will be blood on my hands or the burning ache that consumes me to protect her.

Scowling, I turn back to the bar, throwing the door open with a satisfying crack against the black brick. I storm through it, sulking around the bar to the door of my office in the far corner. Frank's eyes bore holes in the back of my head, but I ignore him and Aramin, who watches me with raised brows and flushed cheeks. Gods, she needs to stop drinking during her shifts. It's pathetic.

Reaching for the door handle, I pause for a moment before whipping around and snatching a bottle of whiskey from behind the bar. Walking into my office, I slam the door shut behind me so hard it rattles on the hinges. The scent of leather and old parchment fills my nose, and I inhale deeply, trying to quiet the raging thoughts and emotions clouding my mind. Stalking past the floor to ceiling bookshelves, I round the large oak desk that sits on the far wall and throw myself down into the worn leather chair, unscrewing the bottle and taking a long pull.

Glowering as the door cracks open, I set the bottle on the table, still holding the neck of it tightly in one hand. Frank peers inside, then comes in and shuts the door behind him.

"Why do you smell like blood?" He quirks a brow at me, shoving his hands into his jeans pockets.

I swipe my hand across my mouth and close my eyes, leaning my head back against the chair. I try to block out the way her skin felt beneath mine, the way her scent burrowed deep under my skin, the way her blood mixed on my tongue and sealed my wolf to hers. Forever. It wasn't supposed to be like this, but the harder I try to not think of her, the louder her screams sound in my mind, pulling a frustrated growl from my lips and tightening my grip on the glass bottle before me.

"Did you..."

My eyes snap open to find Frank staring at me from across the room, waiting, and I sigh. "I bit her. I didn't kill her. Gods, but I might as well have." I take another pull of whiskey, letting the smooth amber liquid burn its way to my stomach.

Frank raises his brows. "Care to explain that?"

"You knew what she was," I say, "and now you know what she'll become. What more is there to say?"

He shrugs one shoulder. "I don't know. Maybe why you care?"

I grit my teeth, not wanting to voice the truth aloud. Because that would make it all real. "Don't act like you don't know, Frank."

He walks forward, lowering himself into a chair across from me and spreading his arms wide. "Got all night, boss."

"Gods, you are annoying." I glare at him, but he only smiles. "She tasted..." My eyes drop to the black label wrapped around the bottle in my hand, and I set it back on my desk, running my fingers through my hair. "She tasted like the first drop of water after an eternal drought."

Her eyes flash in my mind, followed by her scream, and I flinch, leaning back in the chair. Groaning, I bury my head in my hands as I realize what tomorrow is—the full moon.

"Come on, Gideon," Frank says, standing and grabbing my shoulder. "If the change is successful, she'll be back, so no use wallowing in it now. We'll deal with it when it comes, but right now, you need a proper drink. And then a shower—you reek of witch."

"Whiskey absolutely is a proper drink," I grumble, letting him pull me up from the chair as he laughs quietly.

CHAPTER THREE
Adara

STUMBLING THROUGH THE FOREST, I STRUGGLE against the panic clouding my mind. He's coming after me—I know he is. He'd never let me get away. My vision blurs as tears streak down my face. I trip over roots and loose rocks, falling to my knees. My shoulder burns like live flames eating at my skin, and I tear away my shirt to look at the wound.

Two crescents of bleeding teeth marks stare back at me, and I suck in a hissing breath between my clenched teeth at the sight. Scrambling over to a thick tree trunk to hide in the shadows, I use my ripped sleeve to apply pressure to the wounds. I squeeze my eyes shut and hold my breath, fighting back the scream trying to burst from my lips. The sound of flapping wings makes me hold my breath.

"*He's not coming,*" Kaylus says.

My eyes snap open, glancing up to find him on a low branch.

"*He went back inside the bar. No one else came out. I think it's... safe.*" The raven shuffles, ruffling his feathers before tilting his head as he looks me over. *"How bad is it?"*

A hysterical laugh bubbles out of me, and I pull away the bloodied rag to see the bite marks have already healed. Dread immediately fills me as I notice the little silver scars that dot my skin in their place. "How bad? Very. Deadly, in fact." I slump back against the tree, hot tears trailing down my cheeks. I didn't get the money tonight, and I lost what I brought with me, but to make everything even worse, I'm a gods damn wolf.

Growing up as a witch, I was taught to hate the wolves—all of them. It's never an argument, never up for discussion—it's just a fact. We're witches, so we hate the wolves... especially because they were given immortality, unlike us. Or maybe *only* because of that.

For witches, immortality is only ever given by another witch—as a curse or a blessing, but always with the same cost: the caster's life. There've been many witches who fought to find a loophole—like having an ill or elderly witch be the caster, knowing their life is ending soon, but their magic is weakest then. Too weak to be successful. It's always been assumed that we could harness the life of a werewolf to grant our immortality, but it's been hundreds of years, and it's never been proven to be successful. Yet, we hunt them anyway.

And now? They'll hunt me as an experiment to be harnessed—killing me in the process of stealing my immortality—or crucify me as a traitor.

I don't know how long it takes me to stand back up, for the fire in my arm to fade, or for Kaylus to grow impatient. By the time I pick my way back through the forest to the house, the first hint of the sun is bringing life to the sky. I rush around the back of the house, climbing the rope ladder hanging from my bedroom window before gathering it up and tucking it below my bed, out of sight.

I catch my reflection in the mirror of my vanity and wince. My shirt collar hangs limply against my throat, one sleeve missing, leaving frayed edges in its wake, and blood is splattered around the fringe. Leaves and twigs stick up randomly throughout my hair, my eyes are red rimmed with bags beneath them, and dirt is smeared across my cheeks.

I take a deep breath, thankful the house is quiet and that it's only five in the morning. Grabbing some clothes, a towel, and a plastic bag, I tiptoe across the hall and start the shower, making sure to wash my hair twice to get the musky smell of the bar off me, and throw my bloodied clothes in the plastic bag. I finger comb my hair as I stuff the bag under my bed, and at the last second before leaving my room, I grab the bottle of concealer and dab some under my eyes.

Rushing downstairs, I throw eggs into a greased pan and start the pot of coffee. The early morning sun slants through the front windows, casting the kitchen in a warm glow. It's the only warmth in the house—a house that feels sterile with its bare, white walls and polished hardwood floors.

"You're late," she says flatly, walking into the kitchen, looking immaculate as always. Monique's blonde hair is pulled into a sleek bun at the nape of her neck, her penciled eyebrows arched arrogantly over her deep green eyes. There isn't a single hair out of place or a smudge of plum lipstick astray. She brushes invisible dirt off the shoulder of her white pantsuit, then checks the delicate gold watch on her wrist. "Those should already be on a plate. I don't have time to sit around all morning while you play chef, Adara." Sighing, she moves to the counter and fills a travel mug with black coffee.

"They're almost done, Mom." I flip the eggs over, letting the other side cook and the runny yolk harden.

"It's just another day where I'm forced to choose between eating and being on time." She screws the top of her travel mug on tightly, then steps to the table with the blue crystal bowl that sits by our front door. Dangling her keys in her hand, she calls over her shoulder, "Make sure Juliana eats before you go back to sleep, dear."

I grit my teeth to keep from responding with something that will only get me in trouble. Like how I don't go back to sleep once she leaves because someone has to do her never-ending list of chores every day while Jules studies. Or how today I have to do those chores *and* fix this ridiculous mess I got myself into. Instead, I wait and listen to the sound of her car backing down the driveway before moving through the motions of my day.

Five hours later, I've only been able to tackle the floors—swept and mopped daily, the windows—inside and outside glass panes cleaned every other day, the breakfast dishes, and the yard—raked every day there's a fallen leaf invading our sea of green blades, which, in the fall in New England, is constant.

"Done!" Jules exclaims, rising from the long oak table and coming to wave the paper in her hand at me. "Now will you let me help?" She puts her free hand on her hip and stares at me with raised brows, every bit the younger image of our mother with curly blonde hair and sharp green eyes—luckily lacking the arrogance that belongs only to Monique.

I step back from where I've been cleaning the small half window above the shower—one I missed last week after not realizing the downstairs bathroom even had a window and receiving "half a burn" to never forget it again. The small one inch scar is still pink and puckered on my inner wrist from Monique's magic. "Actually, I'm all done. Thanks, though." I half-smile at my little sister, stepping around her to go back into the kitchen and wash my hands.

"At least let me make lunch," she says, stepping over to the fridge.

I laugh and grab a towel to dry my hands, leaning back against the counter. "Right, and if she comes home for lunch, then what?"

Jules slams the fridge door shut and huffs. "You're not my chef or my maid. You're my *sister*. I can manage to cook for myself!" She throws her hands in the air, whirling back to the table and throwing herself into a chair.

"It is what it is." I shrug, knowing there's no use in fighting—neither against our mother or against Jules's justified ideas of what's fair and what isn't. "How about I make bacon mac and cheese for lunch?"

"Really?" she asks, her voice small as she brings her gaze back to me.

I smirk, knowing it's her favorite forbidden meal, too greasy and full of fat for Monique to allow in her house. "Unless you don't want it?"

"No, I do!" She jumps out of her seat to stand by the island, a smile lighting up her face.

"Good, because I secretly made the bacon yesterday so the smell wouldn't linger in the house." I pull the container of bacon from the back of the fridge, then start filling a pot with water to boil. "Why don't you try to turn the knob on the stove to medium?" I glance over my shoulder at her as she moves to step around the island. "Without touching it, Jules."

She ducks her head and smiles sheepishly. "Oh. Right." Moving back to her spot, her eyes narrow at the knob on the stove, and her lips move as she murmurs a spell under her breath.

As far as our mother knows, Jules has been studying every day to become a priestess in our coven, learning the coven's history, the lives of the past and current priestesses, and the common magics they use. But Jules didn't get accepted into the academy for her devotion to the coven. She got accepted because she holds more magic than most witches.

The knob on the stove wiggles for a moment as I set the pot on the burner, but it falls still. It takes her a few more tries, but eventually, squeals of delight fill the kitchen as she sets the burner to medium. I laugh, sharing in her joy, as I go through the motions of lunch before letting my mind wander the rest of the day on what tonight will bring for me.

I keep my eyes squeezed shut, waiting for the house to fall quiet. Voices and movement float up the stairs from the first floor, and I curse Monique's sudden interest in Jules's studies. The one night I wish they'd go to bed early, or at least on time, and they decide to stay up later than normal. Finally, footsteps pad down the hall outside my door and fade as Jules gently shuts hers, and it's only a minute later that I hear the distant click of Monique's door downstairs.

A thin coat of sweat breaks across my forehead. I shouldn't be so nervous after sneaking out the last handful of nights, but anxiety curdles in my stomach anyway. For a brief moment, Gideon Disantollo's face flashes in my mind. Dark curls falling across his forehead, brushing over gray eyes that seem to scowl at everything they see, and a mouth that's tugged down into a frown or a lopsided smile that's mocking. My nerves flutter, and I shake my head to clear it. I shouldn't be thinking of him now—I should be cursing his name for what he's done.

Not many know of the wishing well of Lockwood Forest, but my grandmother used to tell me stories about it from when she was a girl each night as she put me to bed. *"Its magic is beyond your wildest dreams, Addy,"* she'd say. *"It can take away all your pain and bring you the brightest of futures."* Her golden eyes would narrow as the smile disappeared from her weathered face. *"But it can bring great hardship too, if the wrong people find it. If evil lurks within its walls, doom will fall upon us all."*

A shiver creeps down my spine as I remember the warning in her voice. I was only a child then, maybe five years old the last time she told me the stories, but I remember every one, every word. And I remember the way to Lockwood's well.

Slipping from the covers, I crouch down and pull the rope ladder from beneath my bed, then slide over to the open window. I tap three times on the sill and wait to hear Kaylus caw, thankful Monique never believed I had enough magic to call the spirit of a familiar. It's hard to be suspicious of a raven's caw when you live at the edge of the woods and think neither of your daughters could have a familiar—though I'm not sure why Jules doesn't have one. Or Monique, for that matter.

I shake my head to dispel the thoughts, and after Kaylus silently lowers the rope ladder down, it doesn't take long to hike through the woods behind my house and cross back into Silver Wolf territory. Thankful I don't need to edge deep into Gideon's territory, I skirt around to the trees that seem to grow strangely larger, with shadows that feel dangerous and dark.

A shiver snakes down my spine as the shadows seem to swallow me once I step into Lockwood Forest. I clench my teeth, sucking in a deep breath of the chilly autumn air, and glance at Kaylus gliding above me.

"Well?" he asks impatiently.

"Yeah, yeah," I grumble, crunching over leaves as I move deeper into the woods. "Not like I have a choice."

"So, what's the plan then?" he asks, circling above my head. The moonlight glints off his shiny black feathers as he swoops down close.

"Find the well, wish away my wolf, get home. I don't know how long I have until..."

"Until you shift?"

I nod. "Yep." Chewing on my bottom lip, I try to think of everything I've been told about the werewolves, but no matter how much I wrack my brain, I can't think of anything but their feral, primal rage... and their immortality. Gideon is the one I know the most about because he's a constant ache in my coven's side. He lures witches into his territory to their deaths, and he even kills the wolves of his own pack if they defy him... making a message out of every one.

Once, I overheard a priestess talking to Monique about a man—a wolf of Gideon's pack—who had a silver stake driven through his chest. His dead body sat on display outside the Silver Lycans bar for months, and it was all because he questioned Gideon's leadership. He didn't even challenge the alpha.

Another tremor runs through me at the memory of the photograph she showed us.

"When did you start thinking of him as Gideon?"

I jump at the sound of Kaylus's voice in my head, glaring up at him. "What difference does it make if I call him Gideon or Disantollo? It's the same man either way."

He caws in disagreement, and I ignore him as I continue to walk, trying to shake the image of Gideon from my mind.

A sudden, searing pain tears through me, yanking me from my thoughts, and I stumble to the forest floor, loose rocks cutting into my hands and knees. The metallic scent of blood mixes with the smell of decaying leaves and assaults my nose, making me gag. Another wave of pain hits me, making my bones feel as if they're being crushed to powder by a giant. I stuff a fist into my mouth to stifle my screams and pant to catch my breath.

"*Addy!*" Kaylus calls, his talons digging into my shoulder.

My vision blurs as colorful auras burst behind my eyes, but it's impossible to miss the way my fingers lengthen into sharp points, popping and cracking as the bones break. The pain is unbearable, but my panic spikes when Kaylus caws again.

No, no, no! The change shouldn't be happening this soon... Panic sears through me as I realize the change doesn't take twenty-four hours to take effect like I was taught... at least not when it can feed off a witch's magical blood.

His talons tear down my back as I frantically try to shake him off, but he won't let go. Every time I open my mouth or try to form a thought long enough for him to hear, blinding agony rips through me again. And again. And again.

I vomit on the ground, the foul odor making me dry heave, and my arms and legs shake before giving out, smacking my face on the ground. Moaning, I roll onto my side and pull my knees up to my chest. Tears prick at the corners of my eyes, and I squeeze them shut, wishing this nightmare would stop.

I can't be a werewolf.

I'm already a worthless witch with almost no magic. This is only going to seal my fate as an outcast in my coven.

Fire blazes up my spine, and I cry out, feeling my body break and reform. My skin cracks, raw and burning, as fur bursts through my skin all over my body. I lay on the ground, panting, refusing to open my eyes.

A light wind brushes against my fur, and the rustle of feathers, along with a sweet and musty scent, fills my senses.

"Addy?" Kaylus whispers, his beak nudging my cheek. *"Are you..."*

My lips curl back in a small growl, unable to stop myself before reacting to the thought that races across my mind. I slowly open my eyes, gazing at the small raven sitting before me, and sigh. *"I'm alive. For now at least."*

CHAPTER FOUR
Gideon

FRANK LAUGHS AT THE OTHER END OF THE BAR, the same blonde from the night before smiling up at him as she touches his forearm. He hands her two full beers, the froth dripping over the side of the mugs, and watches as she walks away with her hips swaying from side to side. She sneaks a glance at him from over her shoulder as she sits back down at her table, her friends giggling as Frank winks at her.

Suppressing the urge to roll my eyes, I scan the rest of the bar. The card tables are full, along with the bar tables scattered throughout the space, keeping Aramin too busy to bother me tonight, and the dancefloor is packed with bodies. The only spot not overflowing in the space tonight is Frank's bar top. I settle down onto a stool, turning my back to him so I can keep an eye on the crowd.

"Here you go, boss," Frank says, sliding a rocks glass full of amber liquid over. "Your personal bottle."

I grab the glass, sipping the liquor and enjoying the burn as it slips down my throat. "Have you heard from Darrold?"

Frank wipes down the bar with a wet rag, nodding his head. "The kids are doin' good, being their first full moon and all. Darrold's got it all under control."

I nod. Frank had suggested Darrold train the new shifters of the pack and supervise them on their first full moon for their first shift. So far, he's proving to be the best wolf for the role, and for that, I've been grateful. It's one less thing I have to manage myself.

"Speaking of the full moon, did you mention the other shifter to Darrold?"

Looking back over my shoulder, I narrow my eyes at him. "There's nothing to say."

He raises an eyebrow, then pulls the bottle of whiskey out to refill my glass. "What if the council finds out?"

"They won't," I growl. "Who's to say she even becomes one of us? The change isn't always successful."

He shrugs, a hint of disbelief in his expression. "If you say so."

I glare at his back as he walks down the length of the bar to the blonde striding back over. Gritting my teeth, I concentrate on loosening my grip on my glass and push off the stool. Slamming my office door behind me, I shut out the crowd and the noise of the bar before hurling my drink across the room. Glass explodes against the plaster and rains down on the floor, the dark amber liquid dripping down the wall.

That gods damn witch. How am I supposed to notify the council that I bit a witch when I know what she is to me? Because she isn't just a witch now. Because it isn't just a lycan law I broke by biting her, by changing her into a wolf—it's my own pack law to stay away from witches, punishable by death to bite one.

Striding over to the bookcase, I rip the books off the shelves and whip them across the room, each one hitting the wall with a thud before dropping to the ground in a pile.

The wolf council couldn't punish me if they tried—and they have tried. For years, they've despised me, tried to make my life a living hell. But it was hell for me long before they hated me for my power. It was hell the minute the witches came into my life centuries ago.

I throw another book at the wall, the paint and plaster cracking from the impact. I reach for another, but my fingers brush across smooth wood, the shelf empty. Frustrated, I move to the next shelf, stopping when a picture flutters to the floor. Slowly, I kneel down to grab it and frown at the smiling faces looking back at me. A young man—only twenty-two—beams with happiness as he stands beside a beautiful woman with a tiny bundle wrapped in a blanket sitting in her arms. He gazes down at them, his wife and his child, and anger spikes through me. I walk over to my desk and pull the drawer open, settling the photo back into its safe place between the pages of my notebook.

Glancing at the mess of books littered on the floor behind my desk, I huff and stoop to pick them up, refilling the shelf and sweeping up the broken glass. I slump into my chair and lean back to stare at the ceiling. What do I care about the council and their wolf laws? They've only proven to be weak. Unable to hurt or control me, as they wish to keep me under their thumb. Just a bunch of peacock bastards.

And why do I care what happens to that witch? Who cares if the wolf council finds out what she is? She might not have changed anyway. It isn't always successful.

It's always a success with an alpha's bite, my wolf says.

Before I can mutter at him to shut up, my office door flies open, banging into the wall, and I raise my brows in surprise as Frank fills the doorway. "You need to come out here." He turns and moves back out, and I'm left scowling at the now empty bar beyond.

It's not unusual for us to be slower as the night of the full moon draws on, but to be empty? I glance at the clock, noting it's just after midnight. Far too early to be empty under normal circumstances. Though, under normal circumstances, Frank wouldn't be giving me orders. Pressing my lips into a thin line, I move to the open doorway, noticing even Aramin is gone, and I'm hit by the scent of the forest. I lick my lips, my eyes searching for the source of the scent before finding her wrapped in a thick blanket at the bar with her head bowed over a steaming cup.

She lifts her head, and her violet eyes find mine, burning like the blue heat of a fire. "You." Her voice is quiet, and her anger sparks mine to reignite, but she stands, clutching the ends of the blanket around her with one hand as she moves around the bar toward me. "Do you have any idea what you've done? Of course you do! 'Little witch,' isn't that what you called me? But you bit me anyway, and now look at me!" She holds one arm out to the side above the blanket, showing the pale skin of a bare shoulder.

One brow arched, I smirk, shoving down the restless wolf inside me that wants to yank the blanket back up around her until we're truly alone. "And what would you suggest I had done instead? You were caught cheating in my bar, *little witch*. You can't tell me you didn't know better."

Her eyes widen slightly, her lips parting. "I..."

"So, tell me. Why come back here?" I move over to the bar top, settling down on a stool and inclining my head at Frank as he sets another glass of whiskey down in front of me.

"Why..." Her eyes narrow into slits. "You know why I'm here, you bastard. I need you to take it back."

Letting my eyes wander over her, I see the fear mixing with the temper in her eyes, swirling through them like a mist. Leaves and twigs stick up from her thick black hair, but my gaze catches on the scars littered across her skin. Pride swells in my chest when I notice the silver scars at her shoulder, but I clench my jaw so hard my teeth ache as I catch sight of more trailing down her arm, across her chest, disappearing beneath the blanket's edge. "What are those scars?"

Confusion muddles her features for a moment before she follows my gaze to her arms and quickly readjusts the blanket around herself. "None of your business."

Pressing my lips together, I work to control the rising alpha power inside me, not wanting to push her on the night of a full moon when she lacks the practice of control. "You're part of my pack now. It is *exactly* my business."

"I refuse. Now, take it back," she says, glaring at me from where she still stands.

"No." I turn on the stool, grabbing the glass and draining the whiskey in one gulp, then gesture for Frank to refill it, wanting something to do besides think of all the ways I want to touch her.

"No? What do you mean, no? You did this, now undo it." She stomps over and throws herself onto the stool beside me, snatching the newly filled glass from my hand.

Growling, I reach to take it back, but she pulls it farther away. "You're an annoying little brat." I stand and yank the glass from her, draining it immediately.

"And you're a monster," she whispers.

"*I'm* a monster? What do you even know of the coven you belong to?" Whirling to fully face her, I stare down at her small body trembling slightly on her stool.

But to her credit, her spine straightens, something not many of my own pack would be able to do under my glare, and as much as I want to hate it, my wolf again swells with pride.

"My coven is my family. You and your feral pack wouldn't know anything about the true meaning of family."

A sharp bark of laughter escapes me. "You think your coven is more of a family than my pack? Because we have rules? Is a child more loved when they have boundaries or when they're beaten?" My eyes drop to her blanket, to the scars on her arms below its surface, and she fidgets.

"We don't murder our family, like you." Her words are quiet, but clear, pricking against my every nerve.

"You're right," I say, visions of a house fire flashing in my mind. "Your kind only kills the families of others."

"My coven hasn't done anything like that," she argues. "Where is your proof? What families?" She raises her chin slightly, her eyes flashing with rage. "Your kind puts your killings on display like they're a prize to be bragged over, so forgive me if I don't want to join a pack of beasts."

My hand tightens around the glass until it splinters, my nails cutting into my palm along with the shards. "You know nothing of my pack, and now you never will. Get out."

She winces, then her wide eyes glance between me and the door. "I... If I go home..."

Frank clears his throat, and I tear my gaze away from her to glare at him. "Why did you let her in here in the first place?"

"Because she *is* pack, boss. She has the silver scars to prove it. Should I have left her naked and outside instead?" He raises both eyebrows in a question, but all I can feel is the challenge behind the expression and the urge to claw it off his face.

"Go home, Frank," I demand.

He lifts one shoulder. "Can't. Gotta finish cleaning the bar and Aramin's tables. Sent her home along with the crowd before taking this one in," he thrusts a thumb in the girl's direction, as she sits staring down at her hands in her lap. "Figured you'd appreciate the privacy."

"Just take it back."

The pleading whisper steals my attention back to her, tears pooling in her eyes as they raise, glaring at me. My wolf whimpers at her pain, and my jaw ticks. "Why should I? You stole from me. You refuse to answer my questions and have insulted my pack. You haven't even shared your name."

"They'll kill me, and you know it," she says, her voice breaking. "Undo this curse, Gideon Disantollo. I'm begging you! I demand it."

The way her lips form my name has my wolf clawing in my chest to get out, further strengthened in his fury by his need to comfort her. Tears flow freely down her cheeks, and it takes every ounce of willpower not to stride forward and wipe them away, to not gather her in my arms and tear apart whoever gave her the scars marring her skin and caused her pain. "I can't."

"What?" She slumps back against the bar, defeat and horror warring on her face.

Reaching out to steady her, my fingers burn where they touch her bare skin, like thrusting my hand into an open flame. I suck a breath between my teeth, hissing at the pain. "I can't," I grind out, "take it back. Once you're bitten, there is no reversing it." I step back, scowling at the feeling of cold loneliness spreading through my chest as the distance between us grows.

"She's going to kill me," she mutters. Swallowing hard, she looks at the door, as if afraid something will burst through it at any moment.

"Who is? The same person who gave you those scars?" The words are out of my mouth before I can stop them, and I curse myself inwardly as she chews on her lip, avoiding my gaze. Why can't I just let it go? Who cares about this witch anyway?

You do, you idiot, my wolf says. I can practically feel him rolling his eyes at me, and my temper rises.

"Why do you even care? You obviously hate me enough to kill me." She stares down into her lap, picking at her nails.

"I didn't kill you," I say.

"You may as well have." She lifts her chin to glare at me again. "Just because it won't be your fingers stained by my blood doesn't mean it isn't your fault. You put the target on my head the minute you bit me. Whatever hitman does the job will only be doing your bidding."

Sighing, I walk behind the bar and rifle through a few boxes, pulling out a pair of leggings from the box of extra clothing and one of my spare t-shirts. "Here." I toss them onto the clean bar top in front of her, then point at the dim hallway at the back of the bar. "Bathroom is over there."

She blinks a few times before grabbing the clothes and wandering off to change. It isn't until she's in the bathroom and out of my sight that I'm finally able to take a deep breath again. Fucking mating bond. Even if I couldn't see the desperation written on her face, with the bond and her first shift, I can feel it as strongly as if it were my own.

Scowling, I reach under the bar and grab the bottle of whiskey, taking a swig. Frank chuckles, and my upper lip curls back. "I thought I told you to go home."

"Yep, sure did." He continues wiping down a table I know is already clean.

"Are you *babysitting* me?" I slam the bottle on the bar.

"Wouldn't dream of it, boss." He continues on to another table, wiping down the glossy top, keeping his head ducked down and his back to me.

"She's insufferable," I mumble, gaining another laugh from Frank. "She won't even tell me her name."

"Gideon," he turns around to look at me, a smirk on his face, "you never even asked for her name."

"Of course I did," I argue, trying to think back through our conversation. *Didn't I?*

My wolf laughs, the sound irritating because he's just as insufferable as that witch.

"No," Frank says, "you never asked her that. You did, however, ask her many times about her painful past when she doesn't know anything about you and thinks you're a murderer."

I snap my jaw shut and turn back to face the hallway. Gods damn fates...

CHAPTER FIVE
Adara

DRAGGING OVER THE BOLT, I LOCK THE BATHroom door and lean against it, clutching the blanket and clothes to my chest. Inhaling a shaky breath, I bite down on my lower lip as fresh hot tears track down my cheeks. I wish Kaylus was here with me instead of waiting outside. I wish I'd never come here that first night, had never gotten myself into this mess in the first place.

A strange tug in my chest brings a new wave of emotions over me—sadness and fear, but they don't feel like my own. I shake my head to clear the thoughts and drop the blanket at my feet, quickly pulling on the leggings, grateful for their soft cotton against my raw skin. Gideon's scent envelops me as I tug his shirt over my head and braid my hair over my shoulder. The scent reminds me of the whiskey he drank—a little woodsy, a little sweet, and something else that seems uniquely him.

Glancing in the mirror above the sink, I brush the stray hairs away from my face and wipe away my tears, trying to refocus. He didn't kill me, true, but he may as well have. A witch who becomes a wolf is as good as dead. I bite down on my lip, copper coating my tongue, and wince. Grabbing the blanket off the floor, I take a deep breath and slide back the bolt and head into the bar.

As I walk down the hall, I notice him standing behind the bar, glowering at the bottle of liquor in his hand. Now that my anger isn't as fierce, I let my gaze wander over him, taking him in. His broad shoulders are tense, the muscles of his jaw ticking every few seconds, and his black hair is long, hanging slightly in his face. He's tall, not as tall as the bartender, but still at least a foot taller than me. And he's young, though I know he's far older than he appears. That only means he was turned young, and for some reason, the thought makes me frown. His head snaps up, and his light gray eyes find mine. They're a dull silver, the color of clouds on a rainy day. I want to snuggle into him and watch rain pelt against the windows as the world rages on around us.

I shake my head, pushing myself down the hall. Where the hell did that thought come from? I could never *snuggle* the Silver Wolf alpha. I'm not insane, especially after he already attacked me once.

I drop the folded blanket on the bar, deflated from the roiling emotions of the night. I know he told me to leave but...

"Adara," I say, keeping my eyes focused on my fingers as I toy with the frayed edges of the blanket.

"Hm?"

I look up, locking eyes with Gideon as he stares at me. "My name is Adara, but I prefer to be called Addy. You... you said I never gave you my name, so. There it is." I shrug, mustering up the nerve to take a step toward the door. Each inch closer brings another wave of dread. Will Monique smell me? Can you smell werewolf on another witch like the wolves can smell us?

"I'll see you at four."

I whirl around to face him as he places the bottle of whiskey beneath the bar. He keeps his eyes on the rag before him as he wipes down the counter. "W-what?"

He looks up and arches a brow. "Four o'clock. Here. You need money, I'm offering you a job."

"A job?" I look around the bar. The bartender is gone now, and I can't be sure if he's serious or if this a joke... or a trap. "What job?"

Gideon scoffs. "Does it matter? It pays. Fifteen an hour. Now leave before I change my mind."

I open my mouth to tell him it *does* matter because I won't do just any job, but then I snap it shut. I nod once, then rush to the door, bursting into the cold night air and gulping a few deep breaths. Gods, being around him is like... forgetting how to breathe. What is *wrong* with me?

Kaylus swoops down, settling gently on my shoulder as I trek through the forest toward my house. *"Are you okay?"*

I huff. "I guess. D-do you think Monique will smell *it* on me?"

He brushes his beak up and down my cheek. *"No, I don't think she'll be able to."*

Blowing out a long breath, relief floods me. "Okay." I take another deep breath. "I can do this. I have a job now. I can save up the money for Jules's tuition and—"

"A job?" Kaylus caws, and I shush him.

"Yes, a job. He offered me a job, and before you even ask, I don't know what kind of job. It doesn't matter. It pays. Plus, it's at night so Monique should be fine with it, and I'll be able to ask about my wolf. Maybe I can find someone who knows how to break the curse." Chewing on my lip again, I try to think of something. Maybe I could try to hike to Lockwood's well again. Or maybe there's another wolf in Gideon's pack that knows how to reverse this.

Waking up the next morning, I feel far less tired than I expected after only three hours of sleep. Strangely, I feel... energetic. I dig around my room for my headphones and throw rock music on my phone, listening to my favorite songs while I get dressed and head downstairs to start breakfast.

This time, I'm done cooking before Monique is out of her room, and she eyes me suspiciously from the doorway. "What happened?"

I look over at her and smile. "I found a job. It won't interfere with any of my chores. I'll have dinner ready before I leave. And it pays. I'll be able to—"

"No," she says, shaking her head and holding her hand up. Her plum colored lips pull down into a frown. "Eggs, Adara? Again?" She sighs, moving to the freshly brewed coffee and filling her travel mug.

"Wait." I turn and follow her to the door "Why not? I'm nineteen. I've got it all figured out. I'll still study with Jules during the day and clean. Dinner will still be made. You'll even get home before I leave so Jules won't be here alone, just like you want. I thought you'd be happy."

"Happy?" She looks at me over her shoulder, one hand on the doorknob, the other holding her coffee and keys—no breakfast. "Why would I be happy for you to have a distraction from what really matters? If you have so much free time in your life, then there's more around this house you can do. Stop finding excuses to slack off, Adara. You're not a child anymore." Yanking the door open, she slams it shut behind her.

I'm still staring at the closed door when I hear her car back down the driveway. My face feels hot, and my cheeks are flaming. My hands shake, and I curl them into fists, my nails digging into my palms.

"Addy?" Jules says quietly from behind me.

But I can feel the wolf inside me. She's angry. She's challenged. She's demanding to be let out, and she isn't taking no for an answer.

"Eat your breakfast, Jules. It's on the counter. Start studying charms after that. I'll be back in a minute." Throwing my headphones and phone onto the island, I rush out the back door and run into the forest. Kaylus caws above me, but I don't slow down. I race deep into the trees until I stand in a copse of oaks and maples. Panting, I strip my shirt and pants off and close my eyes, letting go of the small bit of control I've clung to.

Flames engulf my body, my skin searing as fur splits it and bursts through. My bones crack and pop, reforming and stretching as I crumple to the ground, digging my claws into the forest floor. I clench my jaw shut, struggling to contain the screams that want to tear from my throat. As the fire fades, I stumble on unsteady legs. The bright morning sun blinds me for a moment, but soon, I'm running through the trees, jumping over roots and launching over fallen trunks. The wind rustles my fur, cooling my body and my temper.

I've never felt so free.

I've never seen or smelled or felt so much—from every critter in the forest to each musty autumn leaf to the soft, wet dirt beneath my paws. My vision is sharper, and my body feels stronger than it ever has before. The wolf inside me is exhilarated, happy. As if she's been a part of me my whole life. As if this is what I've always been destined to be.

The thought stops me in my tracks, and Kaylus caws again from overhead. Whipping around, I run back to my clothes. Disappointment pierces through me, but it isn't my own. I shake it off, peeling my wolf off and forcing my human form back out.

I land on all fours in the dirt, gasping for air, my eyes burning. I swallow back bile as panic explodes in my head. Was my wolf trying to keep control? What the hell is going on?

Quickly pulling on my clothes, I rush back to the house and get inside. I've never been more grateful for the long list of things to clean, a welcome distraction from the last few hours and what it all means for my future.

"Are you okay, Addy?" Jules asks for the third time today.

"Mhm," I mumble.

"You've cleaned that window three times now." Scooting back her chair, she comes to stand beside me. "What's going on?"

Sighing, I sit back on my heels. I can't tell her what happened. It'll only put her in danger, or worse, she'll want to fix it and put us both at more risk. "I... I got a job."

"What? That's awesome!" She crouches down and pulls me into a hug.

I relax into her arms for a moment, wishing I could pause this moment and cry into her shoulder. "I can't keep it. Mom said no." Jules pulls back, her brows furrowed, but I continue, "It's fine, really. It just means I won't have to worry about getting enough sleep each night between work and here."

"That's not funny." She frowns. "You deserve to have a job. You could save up for your own place finally."

Looking down at the towel in my hands, I scrunch my face up. "I was planning to save the money up for your tuition actually."

She sighs. "I don't need to go to the academy. You can't take care of everyone but yourself all the time."

"I know that. I just... want you to be able to attend. You deserve it. You're so gifted, Julesy." I wrap my arms tightly around her and pull her close, trying to keep my tears in. "I want you to be free to make your own choices. To be happy."

"You deserve to be happy too, Addy," she whispers. "And if this job helps you get there, then I'm in."

I grip her shoulders and push her back, narrowing my eyes at her. "No way. You—"

"Yes. I'll help cover for you. You might have to wait until she goes to sleep." She tucks a stray blonde curl behind her ear, a glint in her green eyes. "But we can do this."

I smile, despite knowing how bad of an idea this is, and find myself nodding with her. "Okay, but we pay your tuition first. Then, I'll save for a place."

A grin splits her face, and she claps her hands together, a squeal of delight escaping her. "Deal!"

I laugh, feeling more hope than I have in years because, finally, I have something Monique can't ruin.

As time ticks by, that joy starts to fade the closer it comes to four o'clock. I've managed to work through today's list of cleaning and help Jules study her charms work, along with her priestess studies of our coven's history. I fuss with the ladle after stirring the pot, trying not to fidget, but I have no idea if Kaylus was able to get close enough to Gideon to tell him I'll be late.

What if he decides it's pointless and fires me before I even get a chance to work? I'll lose the last chance I have to save money for Jules's tuition, and I doubt he'd let me back into the bar to ask questions about my wolf. What if she doesn't let me shift back the next time?

I blink back tears as a wave of sadness rolls through me. I rub my temples, focusing back on dinner. Setting the bowls on the table, I go down the list to make sure everything's there—bowls, soup, fresh bread, glasses of ice water, spoons...

"Aren't you done yet, Adara?" Monique walks in and sits in her chair at the head of the table.

I duck my head. "Yes, Mother."

"Well? Go get your sister. Don't just stand there and assume she can smell this." She waves her hand over the table, acting as if I haven't made tomato soup before and it's some horrible potion of poison.

Heaving a sigh, I head up the stairs and knock on Jules's door. "Dinner!"

"Coming," she calls back.

I wait in the hall, knowing Monique won't appreciate me coming downstairs alone after being sent up here.

"Sorry," Jules says, smiling sheepishly when she opens her door. "I missed a question on her pop quiz today, so she made me write the answer down ten times before dinner." She rolls her eyes and pulls the door shut behind her.

We sit across from each other at the dinner table, holding hands in a circle as we pray to the goddesses for our food and our safety, then silently eat our meal.

Monique clears her throat, then smiles tightly. "I have great news, girls." She waits until she has our full attention before continuing. "I've created an internship position at my company for you, Adara. I thought since you wanted to find any old job, this would be the perfect way to build your resume."

Her sweet smile brings bile to my lips, but I swallow it down. "Thank you," I mutter.

"That will give me more than enough time to take your studies on myself, sweetheart," she adds, turning to Jules who pales. She reaches over and grabs her hand, patting it. "It will be perfect. You'll never have to worry about missing an answer again. Isn't it lovely?"

"Oh," Jules says, grimacing, "yeah. Lovely."

Monique's phone vibrates on the table, and she lets go of Jules's hand to answer it. "Hello? Yes, the blue folder... No, Chloe. Honestly, do I have to do everything myself?" She sighs, pushing away from the table and walking into her office.

"You'll still train me, right?" Jules whispers, her eyes wide as saucers.

"Of course I will." I give her hand a squeeze, then start to clear the table. If I'm interning during the day, then I could possibly work for Gideon at night still, but... I look at the sink full of dishes and chew on my lip.

"I'll wake up early and clean," Jules says, dropping plates into the sink. "And I'll clean anything else you need me to when she's at work. She can't spend all day here with me, even if you are interning."

I frown. "She won't leave you here alone. She'll send someone else."

She shrugs. "I'll figure it out. You just need to make sure you get some kind of sleep between the two *tasks*."

"Are you sure? Maybe I shouldn't—"

She turns and shakes her finger at me. "You *should* and you *will*, Adara Morrow, or so help me, I will pray to Hecate."

I raise my eyebrows at the mention of the Goddess of Witchcraft and Revenge. "Hecate? You're that serious?"

She nods once, keeping her eyes on mine, and my wolf bristles at the challenge. "I am, so don't make me do it. Just... be happy."

I swallow past the lump in my throat and pull her in for a hug. "Thank you. This will be great. For both of us."

"What will be great?" Monique asks, stepping into the kitchen and eyeing us both.

"Your generosity, Mama," Jules says with a big smile. "You're the best teacher, and I know I'm going to learn so much from you." She walks over and wraps her arms around our mom's waist, resting her head on her shoulder.

Monique instantly relaxes, brushing her hand down Jules's hair before planting a light kiss on her head. "Of course, my gem." She looks over at me, frowning. "Now, let's go study while Adara finishes cleaning the kitchen. It's an absolute mess in here. I wouldn't be surprised if it took you until bedtime to get everything in order."

CHAPTER SIX
Gideon

SLAMMING THE GLASS ON THE BAR, I WAVE MY hand in the air for Frank. He refills it quickly before moving back to Mila, the blonde who's now a regular in the bar. I scowl at them, taking my drink and heading into my office. I glower at the clock on the desk as I throw myself into my chair.

Five o'clock.

She's late.

Did she change her mind? Unlikely. It didn't seem like she had all that many choices when it came to money and whatever she needed it for. Hell, she took the risk to cheat in my bar just to get some.

Did she get hurt then? I grip the edge of my desk with one hand, my wolf growling at the idea that anyone would lay a finger on her as I try to resist the urge to hunt the woods until I find her. She isn't mine to claim.

Yes, she is, you fool.

I grit my teeth. *No, she isn't*, I remind him. She's a witch, for gods' sake, and I refuse to allow a *witch* to be my mate, fates be damned.

Draining my glass, I scowl at the clock again before forcing myself back into the bar to monitor the crowd. Aramin flips her hair over her shoulder and walks to the bar to give Frank her table's order, swaying her hips with every step and gaining the attention of almost every male in the room. The place is crowded and loud—the night after the full moon leaving everyone energetic and rowdy.

I don't miss it—that feeling of pure release after the moon pulls a shift to the surface. It was freeing at first, but it quickly turned bitter when I realized the lack of control I'd had over it all. It took years to build up a resistance, yet here I am, barely containing my wolf at the mere thought of some witch being injured.

"I knew you wouldn't believe me!" Mila's high pitched voice says, and I glance over to see her swat at Frank's arm with a giggle.

He laughs, leaning across the bar and tucking a strand of hair behind her ear, the touch making her cheeks flush. "I'm supposed to believe some crow tried to fly in the bar in front of your face?"

"No, a raven." She smiles, tilting her head to the side. "And you're supposed to believe anything I tell you, you know."

I appear beside her before I can think twice about it, making Mila jump. Frank stiffens behind the bar, confused. "Tell me what you're talking about," I say.

"Oh, Mr. Disantollo, h-hi," she stutters, looking between me and Frank. "I-I was just telling Frank about this raven that seemed to try to... um. It was nothing, really. It was probably just a silly bird." She waves her hand in the air and lifts one shoulder with a shy smile.

I step closer to her, letting my eyes flash silver, injecting alpha power into my words. "Tell me."

She swallows, nodding quickly. "When I came in the door, a raven came down from the trees. I thought he was going to attack me, but he clawed at the door instead. It was like he wanted to get inside."

Shoving off the bar, I rush to the door and fling it open, stepping into the cold evening air. The sun is setting beyond the trees, and mosquitoes flit around the neon wolf above me. I scan the woods for any sign of the raven, wondering if it's the same one that was Adara's familiar. But why would he come here?

Is she hurt?

I bolt into the forest, ripping my pants and shirt off before loosening my grip and allowing my wolf form to break free. I shake my fur out and sniff the air, trying to pick up her scent, or the bird's, but I can't.

Growling and frustrated, I take a lap through the woods around the bar, but her scent only faintly lingers in the air, and it doesn't go in one direction. Instead, it leads me in five.

But that's not possible.

I should be able to track her, if not by scent, then by the...

Bond? The mate bond you haven't completed? my wolf sneers, cursing me.

Snorting, I pace through the trees, scanning the branches for any sight of the raven, but it's gone. Maybe Mila did make it up, though that feels unlikely.

Irritated, I launch myself through the woods in a familiar direction. Tearing over the ground, I race through the brush and push myself faster until I'm panting, trying to catch my breath. I run until the sun dips below the horizon and the moon rises in the sky. As I reach my destination, I dive into the lake, not caring for the cold temperature, and shift beneath the surface. Pumping my arms and legs, I swim to the bottom, gliding one hand through the soft sandy bed, then push off and gasp for air when I break the surface. I float on my back for several minutes as I stare up at the night sky.

Millions of stars dot the inky canvas above me, and a shooting star rockets across the sky.

This was never meant for me. This calm. This quiet. This beauty. This was meant for *them*, the family in the photo sitting in my drawer. The happy ones with their lives full and their futures bursting with possibilities.

Cursing the fates under my breath, I stalk from the water and back onto the marshy grass, shifting back into my wolf. I take off at another brisk pace, needing the ache in my limbs and the fatigue in my muscles to drown out any thoughts of my past. Any thoughts of Ella and Grace. And any thoughts of Adara.

Buttoning my pants and tugging my shirt over my head, I stiffen as the wind blows and carries a scent—her scent. She bursts from the tree line across from the bar, her hands smoothing over her hair, a wild look in her eyes.

"You had one job, Kaylus. If I'm fired, it's your fault." She glances up into the trees with a huff. "If you couldn't get in, then I'm sure you could've waited here in case he—"

I clear my throat and step from the forest into the pool of white neon light by the front doors. "You're late."

Adara's eyes widen, and her steps falter before she scowls up into the branches. "I tried to send you a message. I..." She looks at me and takes a cautious step forward. "I'll need my shifts to start at this time, not earlier."

I arch a brow. "That isn't how jobs work. I set the shift. I set the pay. You show up and do the job."

She crosses her arms over her chest and looks at the ground. "Well, then, is it alright if I come... um, learn about the... wolf stuff still?"

"You want to learn about... *wolf stuff?*" My wolf radiates pleasure inside my chest, but alarms blare in my head. "Why? So you can tell your coven about our weaknesses?"

Her gaze snaps up to mine, lips parted, but hurt flashes across her face. "Of course not. If there's no hope of returning back to... normal, then I'd like to learn how to control it. I really don't want to be killed by my... for being a werewolf, thanks." She narrows her eyes at me. "And if there's no job opportunity, then I'd like to get permission to still come here to train with... um, the bartender. He seems nice." She shrugs.

"You want Frank to train you?" I watch as she shuffles from one foot to the other and try to tell the jealous growling wolf in my head that it shouldn't matter. It shouldn't matter that she wants Frank to train her to use her wolf or that she was hurt when I accused her of setting us up to be hunted by witches. She shouldn't matter to me at all. "No."

Her brows knit together, and her lips press into a tight line. "No? And what right do you have to tell me no? *You* did this. *You* should be responsible for it, for gods' sake."

"You're right," I say, causing her to eye me cautiously. "I am responsible, and as your alpha, I'll be training you myself." *Because Frank won't ever be seeing you naked again, and I'll make sure of it.*

"And the job?" She chews on her lower lip, glancing briefly up into the trees to scowl at the raven and whatever he said.

"You'll be getting paid to be quiet." I step toward her, and she holds her ground despite the faint scent of fear wafting from her, her crossed arms creating space between us. I lower my head, our breath mingling in the cold night air. "If you tell your coven, any coven, anything about me or my pack, I *will* kill you. I won't lose anyone in my pack because of your kind ever again."

Panic and confusion flit across her violet eyes, darkening them to almost black. "Again?" she whispers.

My gaze drops to her lips, and I force myself to step back. She's a witch. She'll only bring me pain.

Then, why train her? my wolf taunts.

Growling, I turn around and head for the bar. "Let's go, little witch."

She scoffs and mutters, "You can't call me that. That's just asking for your pack to kill me."

Pulling open the door, I hold it open and gesture for her to go in first. "They won't touch you because they don't want to lose their own life for defying my orders. But fine, *Adara.*"

She wrinkles her nose, making her lips pucker, and I fight the urge to kiss her, my knuckles turning white on the handle as I wonder if the touch would burn the same as the last time. "Only my mother calls me that."

I chuckle despite myself and follow her in. She takes a few steps, then stops at the end of the bar when the majority of the crowd stares. Frank smiles and gives a small wave, which she returns shyly. I walk up behind her and lean forward, my lips brushing against her hair, and grip her upper arms gently, desire and disappointment warring inside me when it doesn't sear my palms. "Welcome to the Silver Wolf Pack, *mia fiamma*."

Standing tall, I let my eyes flash silver and survey the crowd. Most are curious, but a few angry stares coming from the gambling tables tell me not everyone is unfamiliar with the witch before me, even if they only know her as a cheat.

"Meet Adara, our newest pack member. Treat her as you would any others in our pack. Touch her..." I scan the crowd slowly, pausing over every angry stare, "and I'll make you wish I'd let you go feral."

The anger melts from the crowd, then Frank raises a glass, and yips and cheers fill the space, welcoming her into our ranks. I step around her, guiding her down the bar and toward the door of my office. I hold up two fingers to Frank, who nods, grabbing two glasses and filling one with water. I bring them to my desk, pouring whiskey in the empty glass and gesturing to the one filled with water for Adara before moving to shut the office door.

"What does it mean? To be feral?" she asks, sitting on the chair across from my desk and looking around at the shelves of books lining the wall.

"Packless. Wolves are pack animals by nature, so to be feral and packless means to lose purpose. Even humans crave community. For us, to be half human and half wolf and then left without that community connection, it means a certain form of torment."

She nods slowly, avoiding my gaze as I sit in my chair across from her. "And... why did you threaten them with that... for me?"

Because you're mine, I want to say—my wolf wants to say. I drink a long pull of whiskey, letting the alcohol warm my insides before answering. "Because I protect those who rely on me, and not everyone in my pack is safe. Not for you."

She chews on her lip before bringing her gaze up to mine. "Can they smell me?"

"They can only smell your wolf, now that you've shifted." I shrug, remembering her charm spell. "But only I could smell you through your charm spell before that."

"Oh," she says, surprised.

"You could use it again, if you're nervous." I narrow my eyes at her. "Though if you're nervous, why haven't you used it before now?"

"I..." She fidgets on the chair, grabbing the glass of water to take a gulp of it, and shrugs. "What are we training on first?"

Leaning back in my chair, I steeple my fingers before me and study her. After a minute, her mouth pulls down into a frown.

"What?" she asks.

"I'm growing tired of you not answering my questions," I say. "Don't make me force you."

She laughs humorlessly. "Force me? Why did I ever think training with you was possible?"

My eyes flash silver, and she pales. "Answer the question. Why haven't you used your spells today?"

She narrows her gaze and lifts her chin slightly, her mouth pressed tightly shut. If it wasn't for the small sheen of sweat on her forehead, I'd question if my alpha power was effective on her or not.

Relaxing in my seat, I release the power's hold on her. "Please."

Surprise colors her face as she sighs. "Fine. I-I have low magic. It's draining for me to use that kind of charm." She avoids eye contact, picking at her nails, and heat colors her cheeks.

"I see. Well, that's... fine."

She looks up at me. "Fine? You're not... disappointed?"

"No. Why should I care if you have magic or not? I didn't change you because you're a witch. I bit you because you're a cheat."

Her mouth drops open, and a smirk crosses my face.

"Now, I want to know who you were talking about yesterday. Who are you so afraid of?"

"That's none of your business." She drinks half the glass of water and sets it on the desk before standing to peruse the shelves.

Frustration spikes and makes my blood heat. "Why do you always refuse to answer me?"

She turns around and arches a brow. "Because it's none of your business. I'm safe, and I'm here, aren't I? No wounds." She holds her arms out to the sides, but her long sleeves hide every scar I'd seen last night. "Are you going to train me or not? Because I didn't come here to be interrogated."

Why should I care? Why does it bother me to not know who gave her those scars?

Because she's yours.

Growling, I push back from the desk and grab a book from the top shelf of the nearest bookcase. "Fine. First, you need to learn pack basics."

CHAPTER SEVEN
Adara

FLIPPING ANOTHER PAGE OF THE BOOK GIDEON handed me, I chew on my lower lip as I read. I can't believe I talked to him the way I did—what is wrong with me? I've never been so outspoken before, so unafraid to speak every thought that crosses my mind. And I can't believe he just let me, either. Ever since he bit me, I've felt torn between who I am and who I've always wanted to be—between the quiet, shy witch who takes the punches and the fiery wolf who strikes back.

I try to refocus on the page before me. So far, this book has only talked about regular pack basics. The alpha rules over the others, each member plays a specific role, and any wolf can challenge the alpha for their status. It even talks about *alpha influence.*

"Were you using alpha influence on me earlier?" I ask, keeping my eyes cast down at the book lying on the desk before me. Gideon has been writing in the books on his desk across from me while I've read, his black curls falling over his face repeatedly, which only makes me want to brush them to the side. *What is wrong with me?*

"Yes," he says, matter of fact.

Glancing up, I scowl at him. "Why would you do that?"

He sets down his pen and looks at me. "Because you weren't answering my question."

"Gods, don't you understand what boundaries are?"

He quirks a brow. "Excuse me?"

"Boundaries. It means my personal life that has no influence on our training or your pack is off limits. And using your alpha whatever to force me to answer you is wrong." I flip the book shut and walk to the bookcases to put it back on the shelf with a sigh, realizing I have no control over the words coming out of my mouth when I'm around Gideon.

"How am I supposed to know if what you're afraid of is something that will bring a threat to my pack if I don't even know what it is?"

I look over my shoulder at him, his hand gripping the glass of whiskey and a crease forming between his brows. "Because I told you it was none of your business, and you should take that as your answer."

"Because you're so trustworthy?" He sets the glass down and stands, coming around the desk to stand before me. "Darling, do you know how long I've been alive?"

I swallow past the lump in my throat as his cologne invades my senses, curling my fingers into fists to keep from touching him, and shake my head.

Leaning forward, he whispers in my ear, "Centuries. All because the only one I've learned to trust is myself."

"Not your wolf?" I whisper, remembering the text. My eyes dart to the glass of water on his desk, the beads of sweat pooling in a ring at its base. My mouth feels suddenly dry, as his body heat surrounds me.

A dry laugh escapes him. "No, especially not him."

Surprised, I lean back and look at him. His gray eyes bore into mine, and it takes all my concentration to form the question I want to ask. "Why? I-I thought the bond was supposed to—"

"The bond between you and your wolf will strengthen your abilities, yes. It'll also make shifting easier and more comfortable. But not all of them are gifted with intuition and instincts. Not good ones anyway." He steps back, his jaw tense, and goes to sit back down at his desk. "The blue one up there is next."

His words bring back the memory of my shift from that morning, when it felt almost as if the wolf inside was... taking control. Glancing back up at the shelf, I pull down the light blue book, thick and heavy in my hands. The pages crinkle when I open the cover, and I notice the writing isn't typed but written by hand. I run a finger over the indents of the text from the pressure of the pen.

"It's the pack log," he says, gazing at me. "Names, job duties within the pack, insubordination reports. Death accounts."

My brows furrow as I scan through the page, then glance at him. "But why would you want me to read this? I thought you didn't trust me."

He leans forward, elbows on his desk, and his eyes darken. "Should I have a reason not to trust you?"

"N-no," I mumble.

"I told you, not everyone in my pack is safe. This will tell you who you are better to avoid."

I want to ask why he doesn't just introduce me to his pack now, show me who I can talk to instead of making me research the ones I shouldn't, but my curiosity gets the best of me. I settle on the floor, leaning back against the shelves and pulling my knees up to balance the book on my thighs.

Frank, the bartender, is Gideon's beta. I should've guessed that he'd be his second. Their bond is too... open, too friendly, when Gideon is so closed off.

Darrold, trainer. My gaze lingers over his name, and I fight back the urge to look at Gideon. *In charge of training new shifters of the pack to help them learn control and develop abilities.* Why would he want to train me himself if someone in his pack already did this job specifically? He could've just handed me off to train with a group.

Mulling over that, I scan the names with entries under the insubordination reports. *Wendell, wife caught cheating. Wife allowed to choose his punishment—all accounts transferred into her name. Anera now head of household.*

His name brings the memory of the greasy cigar man from the gambling tables, and I wrinkle my nose in disgust. Why stay with him at all?

Grady, assaulted girlfriend. Punishment—feral.

Sawyer, abused wife and child. Punishment—death by beating.

I swallow past the lump in my throat, as another entry grabs my attention. *Tristan, caught selling information on pack members to rival pack. Punishment—death by silver stake.*

The image of the man with the stake driven through his chest posted in front of Silver Lycans flashes in my mind, and I bring a hand to my mouth. My vision blurs as I scan the rest of the entries. So many punishments result in deaths, and for what? Why is there no jail, no arrests?

Does this alpha truly think himself a god? To take life so freely? He's every bit the monster my coven warned me of.

"Everything alright?" Gideon stands and walks over to me, crouching down beside me. I flinch away from him, and his gaze drops to the page before me. "At least now you know what I meant." With a sigh, he walks to his desk and finishes his drink, tossing the alcohol to the back of his throat. "I'll get you another glass—"

"No." I quickly get to my feet, dropping the book onto the floor. "I-I'll do it." Rushing to the door, I yank it open and step into the musky, crowded bar, inhaling a deep breath. I inch my way to the bar top, trying to gather my thoughts as Frank closes out tabs and refills beer mugs.

He glances over at me with a smile, and in a few moments, once the crowd thins and disperses back to their tables, he walks over with a water. "How's it goin'?"

"It's… it's fine." I try to smile, but it feels tight on my face.

He nods, picking up a glass from the sink and drying it with a towel. "And how's it really going?"

I rub my thumb along the condensation of the glass, wiping away the fog. "I saw the blue book."

Frank raises his brows. "He showed you that, huh?"

I nod meekly, wanting to leave but knowing I need to stay. This pack is… terrifying, but this job at least pays, and it's the only way to learn the control I need to have to hold on to any hope of staying alive within my coven.

"And you saw Tristan's entry, right?" He sets a mug of dark brown liquid in front of me. I look up at him, and he laughs. "It's tea, love. Chamomile, for the nerves."

"Oh." Grateful for the soothing warmth, I wrap my hands around the glass and let it seep into me. Despite telling myself to be cautious, the words pour out of me when I look into his eyes—full of compassion despite knowing what I am. "I saw him, you know. With my mother. There was... a picture. My..." I glance around the bar before continuing. "My *family* used it as a way to show how... dangerous you all are."

"I see," he says, then sets a hand atop my arm. "Do you want to know what happened? The truth. Not the blue book version, and certainly not your mother's."

Tears prick at the corners of my eyes. How could I be so stupid to want to hear this? This story about death and torture. But I can't stomach being here if Gideon's as much of a monster as I always believed he was, and I hate that the thought makes my heart ache. I feel like a traitor to my coven wanting to know the truth, for even thinking I'd believe Frank over them, but my wolf whimpers and begs me to ask. "Please," I whisper.

"Aramin," he calls. "Cover the bar for five."

The curvy redheaded waitress that I'd seen waiting tables the last few nights walks behind the bar. She smiles at the customers and nods to Frank, but her eyes flash when she sees me. Disgust and hatred flit across her features before she turns back to the crowd with a smile.

"Come on," he says, pulling my attention back to him as he steps from behind the bar and guides me to a table in the far corner, away from the others. "Tristan was around here for a long while. Probably a good century. He was jealous, though. Always challenging Gideon for alpha. Always losing."

Irritation spikes inside me at the thought that anyone would challenge him for alpha, but it's quickly followed by pride that he won every time. Confused, I shove those thoughts away, knowing they're not my own.

"They were close, him and Gideon, but Gideon always held him at a slight distance. Hell, he holds everyone at a distance," Frank chuckles, and the sound, warm and comforting, makes me think of a father I never got to know. "One day, Gideon woke up and was just angry. Like someone pissed right in his morning coffee. He came in here and shut himself in his office for hours. Didn't eat or drink, didn't leave. He'd scream at you if you even knocked on the door, but you could hear him in there, ripping everything apart, throwing anything that wasn't nailed down across the room." He shakes his head and runs a hand through his long auburn hair. "That's when he found it."

"Found what?" I ask.

"The bug. I don't know how he figured out that it belonged to Tristan, but it wasn't long after that when Gideon ripped Tristan's house apart and discovered the papers. Notebooks full of 'em. Mostly about the women of our pack. Their schedules, their partners, their... desires. Anything to exploit them." Frank's hands curl into fists on the table. He takes a deep breath and hesitates. "He was trying to buy his way into being the alpha of the pack a few towns west of here, one that needed a new alpha but didn't have any challengers. It'll happen sometimes, when the alpha dies and there's no successor. But you have to be voted into the position." Sighing, he continues, "He would've won too. That pack doesn't have many women, not nearly as many as they have men, and most of their men come from the state pen, so they don't have any women to... breed with."

Bile twists in my gut. "That's horrible."

He nods. "Gideon didn't hesitate when he saw it. He probably would've just killed him right there if he hadn't seen the girls. Young ones, all the way down to kindergarten. After that, he made Tristan an example. Not just for our pack, though. For every other pack out there, and for the council."

"The council?" I hate asking so many questions, but the book on packs didn't even mention their council. I know Monique had spoken briefly about the wolf council, but being low magic, I wasn't considered an important member of the coven who needed to know about the politics of our world.

He looks past me at the bar flooded with customers. "The council decides what packs can operate and what packs get shut down or dissolved into other packs. They wanted to shut our pack down that year, they have for ages because Gideon is seen as uncontrollable, being stronger than most of the councilmen put together. But Gideon... well, he wanted to show them the meaning of having values." He knocks the table with his knuckles, then stands, nodding his head toward the office where Gideon looms in the doorway, staring at us. "I gotta get back to Aramin, but you can ask him more about the council. He's a good man, love. Just a bit rough around the edges from where the past has dug in its claws."

I stare down at my hands as Frank's footsteps move away from the table, but it's not long before slow steps come closer. I smell him first—caramel and cedarwood and smoke—before I see him step around me and sit down onto the seat to my left. He scoots it closer, and my fingers tremble until I clench them into fists, frustrated that he has such an effect on me.

"I wanted you to be aware of those in my pack, for your safety," he says gently.

"For my safety?" I lift my eyes to stare at him, anger hot in my veins. "You bit me and changed me into the one thing that is sure to get me killed, and you're worried about my *safety*? Have you ever stopped to consider that it's *you* that's putting me in the most danger?"

He presses his lips into a firm line and leans back in the chair, arching one eyebrow. "I can't change what's been done. The consequences were given, and the fates showed their hand. Maybe you should learn to take responsibility for the actions that landed you here in the first place instead of whining about it constantly like a spoiled brat."

I slam my palms on the table, all the fear from before melting away as my temper flares. "A spoiled brat? My life is over, my emotions aren't even my own anymore, and you…" My chest heaving, I scream in frustration and storm away from him. I throw the doors open and burst into the cool night air, my entire body trembling. My skin itches as my wolf claws in my chest to be let out, and I heave gulps of air into my lungs as I try to regain control.

"*Addy?*" Kaylus says, and the tree branches above me creak with his movement.

The bar door behind me slams shut with a thud, and I whirl around to see Gideon lean back against the bricks. "What do you want? To throw more insults in my face?"

He lifts one shoulder casually. "If you prefer."

I scoff, turning back to the woods. I clench my fists, hissing as my nails cut into my palms, and look down to see that they've lengthened into claws.

"I'm more than happy to shift and go for a run together, but if you want to learn control, you're going to have to start telling your wolf no."

Gideon's voice makes me bristle, and I turn back to face him, glaring as he smirks back at me. "You did this on purpose," I growl. "You showed me that book and then pissed me off on purpose."

"You can't let her control the change, or she'll change every time your emotions get away from you. Deep breaths." He shoves off from the wall and walks toward me, setting his hands on my upper arms and leaning in close. "Now close your eyes and focus on your emotions. Your anger, your fear, everything."

He cups my face in both hands and gently brushes his thumbs across my eyebrows, and I close my eyes without thinking.

"Imagine you're putting them into a bottle. All the negatives into one bottle, *mia fiamma*, then think of when you're the happiest. The calmest. Pull that forward and wrap it around yourself like a blanket."

My cheeks flame as I realize this moment, despite everything, is the calmest I've ever felt. I inhale through my nose, leaning into the warmth of his palms. I keep my eyes closed, and once I feel my wolf recede, I step back, not wanting to linger so close to him. I open my mouth to ask him about the name he's used twice tonight, but then he chuckles, the smirk back on his face, and the words die in my throat. It's probably something cruel anyway...

"Good job, little witch. You have more control than I would have expected so early."

CHAPTER EIGHT
Gideon

ADARA WRAPS HER ARMS AROUND HER WAIST, looking over her shoulder into the woods. Her body shivers in the cold autumn breeze that carries her scent to me.

"That's enough for today." I step away from the wall, fighting the urge to fold her into my chest and warm her up.

Her eyes snap to mine. "But—"

I hold up my hand. "No, you're cold and exhausted. Go home. I'll see you tomorrow."

She swallows, her gaze dropping to her feet as she chews on her lower lip. "It isn't like I have much choice." Turning, she heads into the forest without a second glance, her raven cawing loudly before swooping down to settle on her shoulder.

I blow out a breath, forcing myself to go back into the bar before I chase after her. Frank smiles when he sees me and sets a drink on the bar. "Run her off already?"

I scowl at him. "No."

He chuckles, one hand scratching his beard. "Am I supposed to believe you showed her that book just to rile her emotions for a shift?"

Draining my drink, I slam the empty glass on the bar. "I don't care what you think, Frank." I shove off the bar, heading for my office.

"I'm happy for you, you know," he says.

Without turning around, I grit my teeth and throw the door shut behind me. It rattles on its hinges. I storm over to my desk and throw myself into the chair. Happy for me. And what the hell does he know anyway?

I rub a hand over my face with a groan. Why did I show her that book? It only proves everything she's heard of me is true. That I'm a ruthless monster who kills his own pack. Sighing, I know it's for the best. She'll keep her distance now, mating bond be damned.

You're an idiot, my wolf says.

"How much whiskey does it take to make you shut up again?" I mumble.

More than you own.

I finish balancing the accounts over the next couple hours, and by the time I'm done, the bar is empty. Frank and Aramin are cleaning the tables when I step out of the office.

"Can I crash here?" Aramin asks, not even looking up from the table she's wiping down.

I lean back against the bar. "Why?"

One hand on her hip, she turns to face me. Her dark auburn hair is pulled up in a high ponytail, and her black tank top dips low in the front, her cleavage swelling as she pulls her shoulders back. "Because I asked? Why not?"

"Go home. No one sleeps here after hours." I look over at Frank. "I want to do pack rounds in the morning. Let Darrold know I want the new shifters gathered."

He nods, and I go to head back into my office when Aramin grabs my arm, her green eyes pleading. "Please, Dee. Just for a couple hours. I'll crash on the couch in the break room, you won't even notice me."

Pulling my arm out of her grasp, I sigh. "Fine. But when I leave, you're gone."

She pops onto her tiptoes to kiss my cheek. "Thanks, handsome." Then, she walks off, tossing the rag into the wash bucket behind the bar before slipping to the break room in the back hall.

Frank shakes his head, and I roll my eyes. "What now?" I ask.

He shrugs one shoulder. "You know she's just going to be a headache once I leave."

"Don't bother. I already know that." I glance over my shoulder in the direction of the dim hallway. "Remind me to grab a lock for the office."

He laughs. "Sure thing, boss, but even that won't stop a woman from protecting what she thinks is hers."

Throwing a glare at him, I go back into my office, avoiding the spare cot I have stashed in the back for late nights when I don't want to go home. The last thing I need is for Aramin to sneak in here when I'm asleep like the last time. I frown at the memory of her walking out of the office with her hair mussed, in the same outfit as the night before, in front of half the pack.

After Frank leaves, I stare out the window of my office into the dark and lay my head back on the chair. My eyes start to drift close, but a bang on the glass jolts me awake. Walking over to the window, I push the pane open and glance outside to see a brown wolf tilt his head at me. I step back and let him jump through the window inside.

He shakes out his fur, sending his scent through the small space, then shifts. I rustle through my desk and grab a pair of pants from the bottom drawer, tossing them over. Nudity is common among the wolves, given the way of our shifts, but most of us find comfort in some clothing when in human form.

"Allen Rathmann," I say, settling back into the chair behind my desk as he dresses. I reach for the bottle of whiskey sitting in front of me and pour two glasses.

"None for me, thanks." The councilman holds up a hand, then looks around. "Haven't changed much, huh? What's it been? Three years?"

"Five." Picking up one glass, I take a sip.

Rathmann nods. "Right, five. Well." He scratches the back of his head, his short brown hair almost black in the low light of the office. "I didn't come here to chat, unfortunately."

"Mm, you never do."

He laughs, tossing himself into the chair across from me and tapping his fingers on his knee. "Yeah, the council keeps me busy."

Draining my glass, I move to pick up the next one, staring down into the amber liquid. "What did they send you for? Another complaint about my pack being out of bounds? I don't understand what they expect. We need the space more than the other packs. We're larger in number."

"It's about your new shifter, actually." Rathmann leans back in his seat, the nervousness from before fading quickly. "She's a witch, you know."

Raising a brow, I stare at him.

He purses his lips for a moment, then sighs. "There're laws against this, Disantollo. You can't expect us to believe you had no idea what she was before you bit her."

"And if that's exactly what happened?" Adara's face flashes in my mind, a wave of protectiveness following it.

Rathmann's brows shoot up. "If she has enough magic to fool you, then she's far too powerful to be allowed to live."

My wolf growls, and my jaw ticks as I try to rein in my swelling anger. "Are you threatening me, Councilman?"

He holds up both hands before him. "Not you, just the witch."

Setting the glass on my desk, I stand and walk to the open window, my hands clasped behind my back. "If you threaten any member of my pack, that's a direct threat to me as the alpha. Unless the rules have changed?" I look over my shoulder at him, then shrug. "Then again, the council's rules have differed from my own for most of my existence." Turning to fully face him, I level my gaze at him. "I'll be clear for you. Threatening my pack is the last thing you want to be doing if you want to keep *your* life."

Rathmann nods, his lips pressed into a firm line as he holds my gaze. "That isn't a threat to a councilman, is it, Gideon?"

A wide smile breaks across my face. "As blatant as a full moon, *Allen*."

"All this trouble for one witch?" he says quietly. "I'd have thought you of all wolves would want to watch them burn—no pun intended, of course. I know what happened to your family, what, five centuries ago now?"

I step to the side of the window, glaring at him. "Forgive me if I don't offer you the door. It's locked after hours."

Smirking, Rathmann walks to stand before me. "We'll be watching, Disantollo. If you don't clean up this mess, we'll be happy to do it for you. You know, as a *favor*."

Shifting as he jumps out the window, he launches over the grass and lands on four paws. He looks at me over his shoulder, letting his tongue loll out the side of his mouth, before he takes off into the woods and disappears.

I yank the window shut and latch the lock into place, storming over to my desk and launching the glass full of liquor at the door. It shatters, the moonlight filtering in through the window glinting on the broken shards littered over the floor.

Against my better judgment, I pull the cot out, pushing it against the office door to bar any unwanted visitors from coming in. But sleep has yet to find me. Groaning, I toss and turn again, but anger simmers through my body. The gods damn audacity the council has to threaten one of my pack is outrageous.

Even if she is a witch, she's mine now.

Gritting my teeth, I stare at the ceiling. My *pack* now. She's part of my pack, and that means she's under my protection. I knew her shift would trigger her name being added to the registry. I just didn't realize they'd check on it so fast when they've gone years—dozens of years—between checks before, and I didn't know they would know what she was. How did they know she was a witch so quickly?

Scowling at the first rays of the sun breaking over the trees and shining into my window, I sit up and put the cot away. I make my way out of the office and to the back hall, wandering into the break room to start a pot of coffee.

"That's a great idea. I'd love a cup."

Glancing over my shoulder, I watch Aramin get up from the black leather couch and stretch. She looks exactly like she did yesterday, not a hair out of place, and it makes me wonder if she even slept.

She walks up and rests her hand on my arm with a smile. "Thanks for letting me crash here. I can make you some breakfast before you head out."

Shaking her arm off, I grab a mug and pour hot black coffee to the brim. "Nope, I'm leaving now. So are you."

She pouts, crossing her arms over her chest. "Seriously? You won't even think about it?"

"Not hungry." I walk to the door and back into the hall, hearing her heels clicking on the floor behind me.

"You never used to treat me like this until *she* showed up," she huffs, rushing to the bar to grab her purse.

I hold the door open for her, locking it shut behind us, and walk to my pick up truck.

Aramin rolls her eyes. "Well, can I at least get a ride into town?"

Waving a hand at the passenger side, I climb into the driver seat and turn the key.

The engine rumbles to life as she swings the door open, wrinkling her nose at the tattered leather seats. "Are you ever going to get a new truck? It isn't like you can't afford one."

I blow out a frustrated breath and take a sip of my coffee, hoping the caffeine will make up for the lack of sleep. "This one runs just fine."

"Yeah, but it's *old*." She waves her hand around the cab, as if I don't already know how old it is.

"And?" I raise a brow.

She sighs, melting into the worn leather seat. "Never mind. I forgot how much you hate change."

Driving into town takes less than two minutes, and I'm pulling up in front of her apartment before I realize it.

"Thanks," she mumbles, hopping out of the cab and heading inside.

Guilt tugs at my gut, knowing she means well, but I've learned that lesson once already with her. I don't need a refresher. Pulling back onto the road, I drive a few streets over to Frank's. Darrold is already out back when I walk around to the yard, a dozen kids crowding the grass. They all stand up when they see me.

Darrold raises a hand. "Disantollo, good morning."

"Good morning," the kids say. They range in age from ten to nineteen, though most are around fifteen, the average shifting age in our pack.

I incline my head in greeting, scanning the gathered group. "How's training coming along?"

Frank claps Darrold on the shoulder, a smile breaking through his beard as he towers over the slim man. "Real good, boss. They're almost able to control the shift."

I raise a brow, impressed. "Really?"

Darrold nods, pride shining in his blue eyes. "Yes, sir. I've been running exercises with them since the full moon. They can't shift at will yet or hold a shift off completely, but there's been progress. It's the best group I've had in ages."

Looking at the group again, they all shuffle nervously on their feet, and my gaze lingers on the youngest, hidden in the back. She can't be more than eight years old, the youngest wolf to ever have a shift in my pack. Nodding my head in her direction, I glance at Darrold. "She's awfully young. You sure she shifts?"

Her head snaps up, mousy brown hair parting to reveal silver eyes glowering at me, making me raise my brows. "I can shift just fine, sir," she says.

Darrold chuckles nervously beside me. "That's, uh, Jaz. She is young, only eight, but—"

"I'm eight and a half," she says, raising her chin.

"Right," Darrold says slowly. "But she did shift on the full moon, which is why I took her on to train, per protocol. Your eyes are silver, Jaz. Remember what we went over yesterday."

Huffing, she pouts for a moment before closing her eyes. Her lips move while she murmurs to herself, then she takes a deep breath. Once she opens her eyes again, brown irises stare back at me.

I hum, impressed. "Well, Jaz, I see your training is paying off nicely. Good job, Darrold. Keep me informed."

A small smile tugs at the corners of the young girl's mouth, but she lowers her eyes back to the ground to hide it.

"I'll walk with you," Darrold says, his eyes asking permission. His shoulders relax when I nod, and he falls in step beside me as I wave goodbye to Frank. "I wanted you to know..." He glances up at the sky as we get to my truck, his jaw tense. "Jaz, she's an orphan." Scratching the back of his neck, he shuffles back and forth on his feet.

"Spit it out. I don't have all day to stand here and wait while you grow a pair," I say, impatient to get home and get some sleep.

He sighs, bringing his gaze up to meet mine. "She's Sawyer's girl. Mom killed herself a few years back. Couldn't handle all the... judgment."

Lead weight settles in my gut, and my eyes dart over his shoulder in the direction of the young girl. "Who's the guardian?" Our pack doesn't have an orphanage, instead, we have pack mothers and fathers. Those who wished for children but couldn't bear, or those who have the room to take in another wolf pup or two and offer their homes—and hearts.

"Madrona has her, but..."

"But what?" I spit out.

"She's... hard to handle. She's stubborn, outspoken, doesn't listen, and—"

"Is this something I need to deal with, Darrold?"

He grimaces before shaking his head. "I-I guess not, boss. Sorry to bother you."

I give a curt nod and climb into my truck. "Talk to Frank. Or tell Madrona to talk to Frank and handle her own business. Girl seems like she's handling things just fine from what I can see." Pulling the door shut, I start the engine and drive to the center of town toward my house, leaving Darrold standing in Frank's driveway.

CHAPTER NINE
Adara

CLACKING ON THE WINDOWPANE STARTLES ME awake, and I bolt upright to see Kaylus pecking at the glass.

"*Finally,*" he says. "*Get up quickly, Sleeping Beauty.*"

The sun shines bright behind him, and I squint into the morning rays before realizing my alarm never went off... or I slept through it, exhausted after realizing I had to clean the bathroom when I got home last night since I wouldn't be here to do it this morning. Groaning, I bolt from the bed and finger comb my hair, crossing my fingers that it looks presentable enough, as I pull on the ironed white shirt and black dress pants I put out for myself.

I rush downstairs, remembering not to make eggs and starting a pot of coffee before rifling through the cabinets for oatmeal. I chew on my lower lip, then mutter a spell under my breath to make the coffee brew faster, but the spell only works halfway. The pot splutters, steam swirling through the kitchen as the coffee brews hot, then cold and the machine short circuits.

A deep sigh comes from behind me as I watch in horror as sparks fly from the outlet, and I spin around to see Monique standing outside her door, tapping her heel on the floor. "Really, Adara? Now we're going to need to buy a new coffee machine because you're irresponsible—both with your duties and your magic."

Grimacing, I duck my head. "Sorry, I'll make sure I get a new one today."

She walks to the pantry, rummaging through the cabinets, and waves a hand over her shoulder at me. "Obviously. Go get your sister now. We leave in three minutes." She straightens and turns to look at me, her nose wrinkling in disgust. "And do something with that hair of yours. It looks like a bird's nest."

"I'm already here, Mama," Jules says, stepping off the bottom stair. Her face falls when she looks at the steam in the air, the smell of the burnt plastic plug filling the space. Walking over to the coffee pot, she tilts her head, looking at it.

"Don't worry, my love," our mother says. "Adara will buy a new coffee maker today to fix the mess she's made here. Unfortunately, that means no coffee for any of us this morning." She throws me a disapproving glare before sighing with a pointed look at my hair. "Didn't I tell you to fix that mess?"

Jules grabs the coffee pot and pours two travel mugs, whispering a spell under her breath before turning to hand one to each of us. "Actually, Addy almost got it right." She smiles at me. "I warmed it up, and I think your hair looks lovely."

Monique pats Jules's cheek. "Always the savior, my Juliana."

"I hope you both have a great day," Jules says. "I'll make sure to focus on my studies while you're gone."

Monique laughs. "Oh, no, sweetie. You're coming with us. I could never bear to leave you home alone." She pulls Jules into a quick hug. "Now, go get dressed. You'll be training with me in the morning while Adara works, then on lunch, you'll both come home. You to continue your studies, and," she turns to me, "you to catch up on chores."

I nod, relieved I won't be forced to spend the entire day at the office with her and fall behind on the cleaning tasks.

It's less than an hour drive into the city to get to Monique's office, Jules riding in the passenger seat as she quizzes her on the coven practices and high priestesses.

"Batya and Celeste are the highest priestesses in the coven, we govern over the North American continent, and... um..." Jules taps her fingers on her thigh. "And we always have one oracle as a high priestess, which is Batya."

Monique reaches over to pat Jules's hand. "Very good, my love. Why does a coven rely on an oracle?"

Jules looks out the window at the trees racing by, tall pines and maples towering along each side of the road. Most of the leaves from the trees have fallen by now, leaving the pines with their deep green needles easily seen through the forest. "Because their prophecies help us survive," Jules answers.

"And?" Monique presses.

"And they help us hunt the wolves," she answers quietly.

My stomach twists into knots. I know how important oracles are, but I forgot they could divine information about the wolves... about me. It's been over a year since I studied anything about the coven and our practices, since my magic never came into full levels on my eighteenth birthday. Once I was determined to be low magic, I was seen as lesser in any way that mattered. Now, when I study with Jules, I focus on magic abilities, learning spells and charms that will help her magic blossom so she never has to feel as I have—as an outcast.

Only now, I'm more of an outcast than ever before, and if the gods grant Batya a vision, she'll have the prophecy that ends my life.

As the trees become sparse, buildings begin to pop up more frequently until we hit the city. The concrete sidewalks are littered with people, and the tall buildings feel like they're closing in on me. I swallow past the lump in my throat, trying to calm the nervous wolf pacing inside me as we long for the open air of the forest and Kaylus's company. As we pull into the office parking garage, I realize the air smells different here, though it's not something I've ever noticed before. Stale with the odor of exhaust fumes and old cigarette smoke, the air swirls around me, choking me, and I force down a gag as I rush into the elevator behind Monique. I find myself wishing for the sweet scent of cedarwood, then blush at the thought. Only one person smells like that, and he isn't someone that I want invading my thoughts.

Chloe greets us holding one fresh cup of coffee, handing it to Monique as we step off the elevator. "Good morning, Miss Morrow." She holds open the large glass door to the main office, smiling briefly at Jules and me as we pass her. "Adara, Juliana, how nice to see you both."

"Good morning," Jules says with a smile.

"Hello, Chloe," I say before Monique sighs. I've only met her briefly a handful of times, but each time, she's been pleasant despite my mother's temper.

"Adara will be shadowing you, Chloe. Juliana will be with me in my office. I don't wish to be disturbed as I assist her with studying."

Chloe clasps her hands together. "We did have that one property today—"

Monique stares down at her assistant, her heels providing her with an extra four inches over the small witch. "Handle it, then. That is what I'm paying you for." Then, she grabs Jules's hand and tugs her down the hall to the back office, Jules throwing an apologetic look at us over her shoulder.

Sighing, Chloe turns to face me and musters up a smile. "Well, I guess that's the first thing I can teach you." She leads me back toward the entrance, plopping down at the large wooden desk at the front of the office, just inside the glass doors we entered through. Pulling out a spare chair, she gestures for me to sit and begins typing on the computer before her. "So, as the assistant to your mom, the real estate acquisitioner, we look at various buildings and properties and evaluate their profit to the coven."

Rolling the chair closer, I look over her shoulder as she pulls up a list of properties with pictures and various information listed under each address.

"The one we were going to look at today is an apartment building, which is valuable for the coven." She clicks the mouse a few times, pulling up a tall brick building with large windows and a burgundy awning over ornate gold doors. "Not only can we generate income and profit from renting out to the general public, but it's also beneficial for various witches looking to work in the city so they can decrease their travel expenses. We also sometimes will reserve an apartment penthouse for visitors, like the high priestesses when they come into town to check on things."

"How do you determine what's profitable?" I ask, staring at the photo of the apartment building and wondering if I'd ever be able to afford rent for a place so immaculate.

"Well, it's all about the market, really," she says, brushing her light brown hair back over her shoulder. "We have to assess the state the building is in, how much repairs or renovations would cost, and then how much we would be able to charge for rent without being too far over the market. If we're too far out of range, then no one will want to rent from us."

I nod, smiling. "That makes sense to me."

Her knowledge of the market and her job duties, even the duties that sound more like Monique's than her own, seems to be really thorough. I'm still surprised by her kindness, how welcoming she is with me when it's my mother bullying her all day. I know how Monique is—quick to judge, even quicker to condescend. It's one of the things I know Chloe and I have in common.

We spend the next few hours researching the current price of various apartments and looking through photographs of the current apartment building in question, and by nine, my stomach is growling at me for skipping breakfast.

Chloe laughs. "Let's take a break. We've gotten a lot done this morning already."

I follow her down the hall to the breakroom, and she reaches into the cabinet before handing me a muffin and bottle of water. "Thank you," I say, embarrassed I didn't think about bringing lunch or snacks. "I didn't expect to be hungry while I was here. I'm supposed to leave at lunch."

She smiles and lifts one shoulder. "I know, but I always keep extra stuff lying around here in case I work late or something. It's no big deal."

"Thanks," I say again, my cheeks heating. I sit down on the couch and take a bite of the muffin. "Mmm, banana chocolate chip?"

"Yeah, I hope that's okay." Chloe puts her bottle of water down, frowning. "I'm so sorry. I should've asked you—"

"No, they're my favorite! We just never have these at home." I take another bite of the muffin, relishing the sweetness of the flavor.

She blows out a breath. "Oh, good." A ding comes from her watch, and she flips her wrist around to look at it, grimacing. "Crap. I really need to take this call. You good here? It'll be five minutes, tops."

I nod, relaxing back onto the sofa and taking in the comfortable space as she steps into the hall. Black linoleum floors offset the white cabinets and fridge, and a speckled countertop ties it together. The warm brown suede couch is comfortable, and I'm pleasantly surprised to find myself not totally hating this job. I smile to myself and look up as the door swings open, expecting Chloe and finding Monique.

"Mom?" I jump up as her gaze sweeps over me while she holds the door open with one hand as if unwilling to step foot into the same room as her employees. All two of us.

"Is it lunch already, or have you just decided to put as much effort into this internship as you do everything else? Minimal." She looks around the rest of the room.

Chloe appears behind her and mouths, *"I'm sorry,"* before clearing her throat. "Ms. Morrow, hello. Would you like your midmorning tea?"

Monique spins around, her back to me. "When I asked you to have Adara intern with you, I expected her to work."

"Yes, ma'am," Chloe says. "She's been doing a fantastic job this morning, and I just got a call from the apartment building inspector. Everything looks great to move forward."

Monique hmphs, brushing past Chloe and down the hall, back to her office.

Chloe looks at me and slumps down onto the couch beside me. "I am so sorry. I had no idea she was going to come looking for me."

Crumpling the muffin wrapper in my hand, my stomach sours. Leave it to Monique to ruin something the same second I start to enjoy it. "It's fine. If you bring her that tea, I'd bring two cups. One for Jules. Otherwise, Monique will think you're slighting her favorite daughter."

She nods with a frown, standing and moving to the counter. "Good point. I'll do that, and you can go back to the desk. Even if you don't actually do much until I get back, at least you'll look busy." She throws an apologetic look over her shoulder at me, and I try to smile as I make my way out of the room. It isn't her fault Monique sucks, but it stings either way.

After staring at the screen for another few hours, unable to leave the desk, lunch finally arrives. Monique drives us back home, praising Jules on her *amazing growth* after one day of tutoring. "Thank goodness I started teaching you myself, sweetie. Just think how far you'll come by the time you become a priestess."

I roll my eyes in the back seat. *Way to take credit for Jules's hard work.*

"Now, Adara," she says, pulling into the driveway as she finally acknowledges my existence, "I expect you to complete the list I left on the counter while Jules finishes her studying. I'll be working a bit late today, so dinner should be ready by the time I get home. Please remember not to use magic this time. I don't feel like having to buy a new oven *and* a new coffee maker, that I assume I'll be buying myself since I don't see it back there with you."

I bite the inside of my cheek to keep from asking when I would've had time to go to the store to buy a coffee pot when she made Chloe too nervous to let me walk away from the desk to even use the bathroom.

She sighs. "A thank you would've been sufficient, but apparently, I can't even ask for that much.

Don't worry, I'll take it from your savings myself. Go on, both of you. Get inside before I waste the rest of the hour here and have no time to get a meal."

Jules and I are quick to scramble from the parked SUV before she can say another word or threaten to drain the savings that I'm not sure even exists and rush into the house. I groan at the double sided list of chores, but Jules jumps on it.

"I said I'd help, and you already agreed to let me," she sings, grabbing a broom.

A small smile spreads across my face as she dances and sings with the broom, forever like a ray of sunshine waiting to warm my day between the storm clouds of Monique's torment. My heart rate quickens at the realization that I plan to go back to the bar tonight, and with Jules's help with the cleaning, that's actually going to happen.

CHAPTER TEN
Gideon

THE NUMBERS ON THE ACCOUNTS BOOK SWIM before me on the page. Closing my eyes, I press my fingers against them, cursing my lack of sleep the night before. I'd only been able to get a few hours uninterrupted before having to come back to the office.

Looking across the room, I watch Adara where she sits on the floor, glowering at the book in her lap—one about the shift and how to control it. "Does the reading make you angry?" I ask, reclining back in my chair. "Or are you just angry with yourself for choosing that godsforsaken floor to sit on over this perfectly fine chair across from me?"

Her gaze raises to mine, tinged with silver, and she blinks slowly before her expression softens. "The floor is comfortable enough," she mumbles, looking back down at the page she's reading.

"Right," I say, unconvinced. "Then, what has you so pissed off that your eyes are about to burn a hole through my book, silver and all?"

She looks up again, scowling at me. "They're not silver."

Raising a brow, I lift the glass of whiskey from the desk and bring it to my lips, draining it.

Why do you care? my wolf asks, laughing.

"Do you ever drink anything else, or are you enjoying being an alcoholic who runs a bar? Seems like a precarious situation to me." She purses her lips to the side, the hint of a dimple appearing in her cheek.

"I don't see the point when nothing else dulls the world to manageable." Refilling the glass, I leave it on the desk.

She narrows her eyes at me. "Are you going to take me around the pack at all? Or outside to practice my shifting without pissing me off under false pretenses first?"

I laugh humorlessly. "Are you out for a good adrenaline rush, *mia fiamma*? Because going around the pack is only asking for trouble when the wolf council already knows of your existence."

The color drains from her face, and her lips part. "The... what? They know I'm a new shifter or..." She swallows, glancing over at the dark forest beyond the window.

"They know what you are, little witch, and I'd like to know how." I level my gaze at her, suspicion crawling over my skin and rolling through my gut.

Her eyes snap to mine, her eyebrows practically in her hairline. "You think it was me?"

"I have zero reasons to trust you. The only other one to know about this is Frank, and I know he'd never cross me."

A dry laugh escapes her lips as she tosses her head back. "You think I told the wolf council what happened. Oh, that's rich. Gideon Disantollo, Silver Wolf Pack alpha, can run his own bar and has been alive for *centuries*, but is so stupid he thinks I'd offer my own life on a silver platter to wolves."

Clenching my jaw, I slam my palms on the desk, making her jump. "Don't insult me. There's three of us who know, and you're the only one I don't trust. You're the one who would benefit from them dismantling my entire pack."

She throws the book she was reading at me, and I dodge it, anger flaming through me. "You think I'm an idiot then? Who cares about you and your stupid pack when it's *my life* in danger, you asshole?" Turning around, she stomps to the door.

Before she can yank it open, I use my speed to beat her there, planting my palm on the wood and keeping it firmly shut. Leaning down, I whisper in her ear, "I don't trust your kind, I never will, but I will find out it was you that tipped them off. And I'll kill you for opening your mouth and failing at the one job you're being paid to do."

Turning her head to the side, she glares into my eyes, her violet irises swallowed up by silver. Her lips are a breath away from mine, and I fight back my traitorous wolf, whining to lean forward and kiss her. "You won't find anything but your own trust issues staring back at you. I don't know—and I don't care—what the wolf council will do to you, but I'm only here because I'm trying to save my own life," she spits. "Now I have the wolf council after me, who I'm sure wants to see me killed, right? Whatever they want from you, it can't be worse than that."

Irritated, I glare down at her. How does she not know it's a death sentence to turn a witch, not just be the witch who was turned?

Because she didn't do it, my wolf says. *You're just being an ass.*

Growling, I stalk back to my desk, desperate to create space between the raven haired witch and myself. It's hard enough to be in the same room as her, but to be so close, to inhale her scent and feel her warmth, it's unbearable.

She whirls around, leaning back against the door with her arms crossed over her chest. "You don't even trust the council that governs you, but you trust Frank's loyalty so much that you wouldn't even question him and believe I'm suicidal, just to get your pack shut down." Narrowing her eyes at me, she adds, "Why am I here, Gideon? Why is it so important for you to train me yourself when you can't stand to be near me?"

My jaw is so tight my teeth ache. Raking my gaze down her body, my eyes catch on every curve. The way her black leggings hug her hips and the tight t-shirt stretching over her chest. "Why are you such a bitch tonight? What crawled up inside you to die, Adara?"

She flinches at her name, glaring at me from the door. "Screw you."

"I thought all witches were relatively well off. Taken care of by their covens. So, why are you here? Why do you need money?"

Pulling on the door, she flings it open, and it slams into the wall. She stalks out into the half full bar, and I watch her go, torn between chasing after her and letting her leave.

Rathmann might be waiting for her.

Growling in frustration, I know my wolf is right, and I launch myself after her, following her into the cold autumn night outside. The second the door shuts behind me, she whirls around. "My life is none of your business!" she yells, throwing her hands in the air. "I don't know what happened to you. I don't know what the witches have done to you. But it wasn't me! Stop asking me what happens outside of these *shifts*, and stop blaming me for the pain you're clinging to like a life vest."

I open my mouth, angry and ready to yell back, when she lets out a frustrated cry and reaches down to grasp the hem of her shirt. My mouth goes dry as she pulls it over her head and hurls it at the ground, my groin tightening. She strips down quickly, throwing herself into the woods as the sound of cracking bones fills the air.

My wolf claws at my chest, and for once, we want the same thing. I barely get my clothes off before he bursts through, the shift happening quickly. I lunge into the forest, chasing after her. Her fur, as black as my own, calls to me like a shadow recognizing its darkness in another. My paws slam against the ground, pushing me faster. I'm panting by the time I catch up to her, exhilarated at the challenge her speed brings me, something I've rarely felt before.

We run like this for hours, and I'm surprised to realize I'm enjoying my wolf and the freedom running brings me. The fresh air, the night sky, the trees... the she-wolf running beside me. Every so often, I glance over at her, wanting to say something but refusing to break the silence first when her words still echo in my mind.

"I'm sorry," she says, her voice breaking through my thoughts and making my heart race.

Why does speaking with her like this feel even more intimate—more dangerous?

Her pace slows, and reluctantly, I follow her lead, slowing down and turning to face her. Her chin is tilted up, her eyes on the moon above us. *"I shouldn't have said what I did. It was cruel."*

Padding closer, I sit beside her, my fur brushing against hers and sending shivers down my spine. *"What happened?"*

She huffs. *"I just had a bad day. I'm... I'm ready to go back now."*

I look over at her, her silver eyes like two stars against her dark fur. I want to push, to ask her about her day, to make her answer me, but my wolf is stronger in this form. He refuses. Raising my chin back to the moon, I howl long and deep. After a few moments, her howl joins mine, and a piece of my soul ignites like a fading ember being reintroduced to the flames as I listen to the melody between us.

Taking off into the woods, I run, knowing she's following me. I weave my way through the trees, jumping over logs and darting through the brush. It isn't long before we reach the lake. I don't look back, shifting as I launch myself into the water, sinking below its cold surface. Another splash sounds beside me, and her fingers wrap tightly around my forearm, her nails digging into my skin. We break the surface, and she gasps.

"Oh my gods, this water is freezing!"

I grab the arm still holding me, pulling her shaking body to mine without thinking. I use one arm to tread water as the other wraps around her waist, pressing her to me. Her wide eyes stare up at me, violet and beautiful, her hands splayed across my bare chest, and before I can tell myself no, I lean down and claim her mouth as mine.

I tighten my arm around her, holding back the urge to devour her completely, but she moans softly into my mouth, her hand gliding up my chest to bury into my hair. She pulls me closer, deepening the kiss, and my mouth moves over hers, my tongue darting out to her lips, licking along the seam until she opens and grants me entrance. A growl rumbles from my throat as I taste her—faintly sweet as tree sap.

My chest tightens, like a cord being pulled taut, and she pulls back with a gasp, her fingers touching her swollen lips. Panting, we stare at each other, and I want to tear my eyes away from her but also pull her back to me because I wasn't done. I'm not done tasting her. I'm not done feeling her wet, naked body against mine, her bare skin beneath my fingers.

"Warmed up now?" I say, my voice breathy even to my own ears, then immediately curse myself for being an idiot.

"What?" she asks softly, her brows furrowing.

Don't say it again!

"You were shivering," I shrug, smirking, "so I wanted to make sure you were warmed up now."

Realization dawns over her face, and her cheeks flame scarlet in the moonlight. "You're a bastard." She shoves away from me, swimming to shore and wrapping her arms around herself as she stands trembling on the grass.

Following her, I swallow past the lump in my throat, watching as she mutters to herself.

"Why won't you come out? Am I not angry enough for you?" Her mouth twists into a grimace.

I plop down on the marshy bank. "If you're trying to shift, it won't work."

Her eyes snap open and glare at me. "Well, tell me how to do it. That's what you agreed to do. Train me. Not," she glances at the rippling surface of the lake, "other things."

I chuckle under my breath, disappointment warring inside me. "Maybe you didn't feel it."

She looks at me suspiciously. "Feel what?"

I wave my hand in the air between us, avoiding her gaze. "The bond between us. Your wolf won't want to leave mine, no matter how angry you are."

Rubbing the center of her chest with one hand, she swallows, fear tainting the air between us.

"So, you did feel it," I mutter, earning another glare from her.

"What did you do?" she demands, her voice shaking slightly.

Raising my brows, I lean back on my hands and gaze up at her with a smile, forcing my eyes to stay on her face and off her perfectly naked body. "Me? Nothing you don't already know about, darling."

"Teach me how to shift. I want to go home." Her lips tremble—from the cold or something else I'm not sure.

"I already told you it won't work."

Silver flashes in her eyes. "Tell me why! Fix it. Whatever this mess is between us, just make it go away."

I get to my feet, towering over her as I step closer. I cup her jaw with one hand, my fingers brushing the wet hair at the nape of her neck, and bend my head down. "You think I want this?" I whisper. "You think I want to mate with some witch with no powers who can't even control her own wolf?"

"What are you talking about—mates?" Her hands push against my chest, creating space between us that feels like a canyon.

I laugh humorlessly. "Mates, Adara. You must be familiar with the term, even slightly. Each wolf only finds one mate in their lifetime—destined by the fates, of course." I spread my arms wide before her. "What a destiny, right? You get the alpha's power and strength, and I get you—powerless little witch that you are."

Pain clouds her eyes. "You're every bit the monster I thought you were."

You're an asshole.

The trees rustle behind us, and that damn raven caws, circling the air above us. "Take me home, Kaylus," she says, brushing the tears from her cheeks.

Clenching my jaw, I lay down onto the grass and stare up at the sky. My wolf whimpers, pacing inside and clawing to get out and go after her. But I meant what I said—what good is an alpha's mate if she isn't powerful?

Because you love her. Because the bond will—

"Shut up, you miserable sack of fleas," I mutter, scowling at the stars above me as they mock me, reminding me of her wolf's eyes. I rub a fist over my chest, feeling the vaguely painful tug of the bond as she moves away from me. Gods damn it all...

CHAPTER ELEVEN
Adara

"MATES?" KAYLUS ASKS, DROPPING MY CLOTHES at my feet after gathering them from outside the bar.

Sighing, I curse my wolf for forcing me to shift and then hiding when I'd needed her. With the fear of the wolf council, and my anger at Gideon for thinking so low of me, all after dealing with Monique, it was barely containable. I'm surprised I even got all my clothes off before she came bursting out of me.

"And you're sure the wolf council knows?" he asks.

I close my eyes, counting to five before I answer him to try to keep my emotions in check. "Yes, *mates*. I- I felt it. It was undeniable—like a cord snapped tight between us the moment our lips met." I pull on my shirt, tugging it down over my leggings as my chest begins to ache. I try to ignore the pain as I walk away from him, but it increases with every step I take, raising my panic along with it. "And no, I don't know for sure since I don't have any proof, but Gideon seemed pretty convinced." I say a silent prayer to the gods above that he's wrong—that we aren't mates, because I can't be a wolf *and* mated to the alpha. That's too cruel a fate, even for the gods.

The walk back to the house is quiet. For once, Kaylus seems to be lost in his own thoughts, or maybe he's as lost in mine as I am. Climbing up through my window, I rub my eyes, excited to fall under the covers when a piece of paper lying on my pillow catches my eye.

Addy,
Mama made me write sentences all night, and I could only clean the upstairs for you after she caught me sneaking downstairs. I'm sorry. I'll wake up early to help finish cleaning or cook breakfast—whatever you need.
—Jules

Groaning, I walk over to my desk and look at the double sided cleaning list Monique left for me. Jules and I were able to do almost half of it before dinner yesterday, and she was able to do another section by cleaning the upstairs for me last night, but that still leaves three or four tasks left. I glance over at my clock, realizing I have to be awake in four hours to start breakfast and coffee before going back to Monique's office.

After finishing the list, I sit down at the kitchen table and rub my eyes while the coffee starts to brew. It doesn't feel like I've done anything but blink my eyes a few times before I hear someone clearing their throat loudly.

Bolting upright in my seat, I rub a hand over my face, realizing I fell asleep on the kitchen table. The scents of oatmeal and fresh coffee fill my senses, and I look up to find Monique staring at me with Jules wringing her hands behind her.

"If I thought it was Juliana's responsibility to cook, I'm sure I would've made that perfectly clear. We leave in five minutes, so I suggest you clean yourself up. You look like you just walked through a tornado, and you smell like filth." She turns up her nose with a raised brow and spins on her heels toward her room, a bowl of oatmeal in one hand.

Jules rushes forward, whispering an apology under her breath. "I'm so sorry. I tried to let you sleep a little bit since you seemed so tired. I didn't expect her to get up extra early. I—"

I put my hand on the top of her head and try to smile. "It isn't your fault. I was tired, and you were trying to be your sweet self." Covering a yawn with one hand, I walk past her to the stairs to go get ready.

Keeping myself awake during the drive to the office is harder than I anticipated, and the only thought that keeps creeping into my head is the memory of last night's kiss... and what he said after that.

"Warmed up now?"

I scoff at the memory and sink lower on the backseat.

"Do you have something to say Adara?" Monique looks at me in the rearview mirror, her lips pressed firmly together.

"No, Mother," I mumble.

She sighs. "Sit up straight, and please stop mumbling. You know how I hate when you mumble. You either have something to say or you don't. Don't mumble because you can't decide."

My jaw ticks as I suppress the urge to roll my eyes. "No, Mother," I say, my tone clipping each word.

"I expect you to do some actual work today," Monique says when we park the car and head into the elevator. She glances back over her shoulder at me. "That means no breaks when you're only here for half a day in the first place."

She turns back around without waiting for a response and swiftly steps off the elevator when the doors open, pulling Jules along behind her as she sweeps past Chloe and heads down the hall to her office. Heaving a sigh, I walk over to Chloe and plaster a smile on my face. "Good morning, Chloe."

She pulls her attention from the now empty hall and smiles back at me. "Good morning! Come on, I have some new updates on that apartment complex from yesterday."

WHITNEY MORSILLO

Sitting at Chloe's desk, we've been able to go over the appraiser's report of what will be needed and gather notes on the market for the current available apartments for rent. Three cups of coffee later, and I'm only mildly exhausted.

"I'm going to run back and drop off this proposal for purchase to Monique, okay?" Chloe grabs the paper off the printer and stands.

I nod, resting my chin in my hand as I lean forward on the desk. A yawn escapes me, and I glance over at the computer screen, realizing that it's time to leave. I grab my coffee mug and bring it to the breakroom, washing it in the sink before drying it and replacing it in the cabinet. As I open the door to head back to the desk, Chloe rushes out of Monique's office, pulling the door tightly shut behind her.

I wait as she walks toward me, and she jumps when she glances up from the floor. "Oh, Adara, I didn't see you there." She gives a small smile and glances back at the office door.

I follow her gaze, then look back at her, noting the tightness around her eyes. "Is everything okay? I thought it was about time to leave for lunch."

"Oh... um, well, apparently, Ms. Morrow has an important meeting right now, so she's asked to not be interrupted."

Following Chloe to her desk, my stomach sinks. "Do you know how long she'll be? I-I just have stuff I need to get done at home is all."

She shakes her head, chewing on her lower lip. "No, sorry," she whispers.

I spend the next two hours glancing at the clock every two minutes and fighting the growing heaviness of my eyes as Chloe goes over her usual afternoon tasks.

"Are you okay?" she asks.

I blink a few times and try to hold back a yawn. "Yeah. I'm tired, but I'm okay."

"If you're so tired, then I don't see why you wanted to work so badly." Looking up from the computer, I see Monique and Jules standing off to the side in the hall, Monique's stilettos replaced with ballet flats allowing her to walk soundlessly.

"I'm not sleeping on the job, Mom. Is it time to leave, or would you like me to take a break with Chloe for lunch?" I smile sweetly, knowing the question is only going to goad her.

"Honestly, Adara, your work ethic is deplorable. Never wanting to stay, constantly wanting to take a break. When are you ever going to put some effort in so you can learn how to support yourself?"

Sighing, she adjusts the strap of her purse on her shoulder and turns toward the glass doors.

Standing from the desk, I wave goodbye to Chloe and follow Monique and Jules to the elevator. My leg bounces anxiously the entire drive home. When we pull into the driveway, I burst from the backseat and rush inside, grabbing the new, tedious list of chores and making a mental note of what I can cook for dinner that will need the least prep time. It isn't until the door swings shut behind me that I look up and realize Monique got out of the car with us.

"You're staying?" I blurt out, silently cursing myself for my lack of self-control.

She raises her brows at me. "Do I need your permission to come home early?"

"N-no..."

"Enough with the mumbling, Adara," she snaps. "Come, my gem, let's finish your studying now that I don't have any meetings for the rest of the evening." She grabs Jules's hand, who throws an apologetic look over her shoulder as she trudges toward Monique's office.

Storming over to the fridge, I grab a cheese stick and stuff it into my mouth as I start on the first task, realizing there's ground turkey meat that I can use to make meatloaf for dinner. Quick prep, and oven baked—perfect.

"Adara," Monique calls. "Don't forget to fix lunch. Now, please!"

Closing my eyes, I blow out a frustrated breath. "Yes, Mother," I call back, going back into the fridge to grab the ingredients for sandwiches. She'll hate how lazy this is, but right now, I just don't care. I have so much cleaning to do, and I was really hoping to be done after dinner so I could get a couple hours of sleep before going to the bar.

Chewing on my lower lip as I smear mayonnaise over the pieces of bread, I think about how what I really want is to skip sleep again to search for Lockwood's well. If I could wish away my wolf, then this whole problem would be solved... right? No wolf, no mate bond. I could go back to my coven—back to my life.

My wolf whines inside my head, anxious at the thought of a life without Gideon, and I shove the thought to the back of my mind, knowing that I'll probably regret not taking that nap tomorrow. After bringing the sandwiches to the office, I slip outside to rake the yard. The warmth of the sun warms my skin, and the soft breeze keeps me cool. I hum to myself, watching for Kaylus in the branches as I gather up the fallen leaves and inhale the sweet scent of crisp autumn air.

Branches creak at the edge of the yard, and I glance over to see my raven sitting in the shadows, high up on the pine tree. I let the thoughts of Lockwood's well flow through my mind quickly.

"*Tonight?*" he asks, and I give a small nod, ignoring the wolf pacing inside me at the thought of losing our connection—and our mate. Who wants a powerless little witch for an alpha's mate, he said, but why would I want a heartless monster like him for the rest of my immortal life? I wouldn't. I *don't*.

Pushing aside my panicked thoughts of being stuck with him for the rest of eternity, I rush through most of the list before dinner and struggle to stay awake while scrubbing the baseboards after tossing the meatloaf into the oven. The savory smell of the meal permeates the air, and my stomach growls. We eat in silence as Monique surveys the house between bites of food.

"You *cleaned* the baseboards?"

"Yes," I say, frustration brewing in my chest at her tone. It took me thirty minutes just to do that one thing.

"Hm," Monique says, rising from her seat and swiping a finger across the windowsill behind us. "But you forgot the windowsills because, of course, you did." She sighs, turning toward her office.

I lick my lips. "But... the windowsills weren't on your list."

She turns to face me when she reaches the doorway. "Am I supposed to list everything out for you like you're a child? Is that the only way you're able to see what's dirty, Adara?"

She pulls the door shut behind her, leaving me staring at the white wood from the dinner table. I grab my plate and hers, storming to the sink and throwing them down before closing my eyes and counting to five. Then, ten. Then, twenty. But my skin itches, and my wolf is clawing to get out.

"Addy?" Jules's soft voice is full of concern and breaks through my haze.

"It's fine. I'll clean up dinner, then tackle the sills. I... I just will go to bed a bit later than you tonight is all." I throw a small smile over my shoulder at her, seeing her furrowed brows and her lips turned down. "It's fine, Jules. I promise. Go ahead and get ready for bed, okay?"

Jules looks at the closed office door, knowing our mother is still awake, most likely listening to our conversation, then her shoulders slump as she heads up the stairs to her room.

Finishing up the last chore, I flick the lights off and slowly climb the stairs, stifling a yawn. I change out of my outfit and into leggings and a t-shirt before moving to the window and tapping on the sill.

Kaylus flies over and brings the rope down, allowing me to climb down to the yard and make my way across to the forest's edge toward Silver Lycans.

"No well tonight, then?" Kaylus asks, cawing overhead. *"No sleep, either?"*

I rub a hand over my face, trying to wake myself up. "No sleep. No well. I had to finish that chore's list and a couple things that weren't even on it."

"She's giving you secret tasks now?"

I scoff, the memory of Monique standing in the doorway looking at me like a helpless, irritating toddler. "Pretty much."

As the bar comes into view, I linger in the tree line. A blonde woman I recognize as a regular bursts from the bar with a couple of friends, giggling and blushing. They stumble away from the door as one of them lights a cigarette.

"Isn't he just so cute?" the blonde says, a smile stretching across her face as she looks dreamily back at the bar doors.

One of her friends, taller with dark brown hair, barks a laugh. "Don't you always think he's cute, Mila? You practically drag us here every night just to drool over him."

Hot jealousy sears through me, wondering if they're talking about Gideon. But I shake my head to clear the thought. He isn't mine to claim. I don't even want him.

"Shut up, Cali!" Mila, the blonde, says, as both her friends laugh. "Frank is just... sweet. And cute!"

My body relaxes when I hear the bartender's name, and I step from the trees finally, heading toward the bar. Even if they were talking about Gideon, I wouldn't care. I don't even want to be alone with him after last night. My heart aches at the memory, and I clench my fists before grabbing the door and whipping it open.

CHAPTER TWELVE
Gideon

FRANK POURS ANOTHER ROUND OF BEERS AS the band gears up to start another song, and I follow his gaze to Mila's tight jeans as she sways to the door and slips outside with her friends. Huffing, I lean back against the wall by my office door and check the time. Again.

Glancing at the other end of the bar, I hold my breath as the door opens and a dark haired woman in leggings steps inside. My heart rate picks up when her scent wafts in my direction, and my groin tightens at the memory of her skin beneath my hands, her lips against mine.

My wolf growls, reminding me of the way the night ended, and I shake the thoughts from my mind as I push off the wall to approach her, annoyed at the fact that I've been waiting for her to get here instead of working.

"You're late," I say, as she stands near the bar without moving.

She lifts a brow at me. "And?"

I press my lips together, curious by her short remark and the dark circles under her eyes—and irritated all the same. "Is everything alright?"

Pushing past me, she scoffs. "Don't pretend like you care." I follow her along the length of the bar and into my office, where she plucks the book she was last reading from the shelf and turns to go back into the bar area.

"What are you doing?" I follow her to an empty table in the back of the room where she sits down and opens the text before her. I hate following her around like this, like some lovesick puppy unable to tear himself from his new plaything's side.

Looking up slowly at me, she narrows her eyes. "What does it look like I'm doing, Gideon?"

"Why are you out here?" I wave my hand around at the bar—loud and crowded. "You can't possibly read that in here."

"Why do you care? I'm studying. I'm staying quiet, *as I'm being paid to do.* Powerless little w—" She looks around us briefly, then sighs. "Just go. I know you don't care. It's just about *control*, and I'm tired of the games."

Clenching my jaw, I inhale through my nose and try to relax my shoulders. "I'm not playing games with you, Adara. I don't see why you're out here trying to read when—"

Bringing her gaze down to the book before her, she cuts me off, "I will not be alone with you again."

Growling, I curse under my breath and stalk back to the bar, throwing myself onto a stool.

Did you honestly expect it to go any different? my wolf mocks.

I toss back the glass of whiskey Frank sets before me, ignoring his raised brow as he moves to refill it. Insufferable little witch. She could've gone into the office and told me to leave if she didn't want to be alone with me—

You wouldn't have listened.

She didn't even give me the chance! Instead, she sits out here, reading a book in a noisy bar with all these men watching her. I can practically feel their slivering gazes and hear their drool pooling on my floors.

An hour passes, and somewhere along the way, Frank switches my drinks from full whiskey to watered down. I scowl at him as I lift my fourth one, then turn and watch Adara studying at the table alone. Her chin rests in one hand, her elbow propped on the table and her hair hanging like a curtain across her face until she reaches up to tuck it behind her ear. A strand comes loose and falls back into her eyes, and the urge to walk over and brush it aside is almost unbearable. I'm halfway out of my stool when the band announces that they're taking a break, and the lead guitarist—Keith, a young wolf who recently joined my pack a couple decades ago—walks over and sits down across from her.

Dropping back onto my stool, I drain the rest of the watered down, sorry excuse of a drink and slam it on the bar to watch.

Keith smiles, his mouth tugging to one side. "Hey, are you new here? Shit, that was a dumb thing to ask." He laughs and scratches the back of his head. "Well, I'm Keith. I'm not new here, but I am part of the band that plays here each night. I haven't seen you around before, though. Do you come here often? Damn it, sorry, that was a cheesy pick up line."

Adara throws her head back laughing.

Gods, I want to make her laugh like that.

I grit my teeth together and push the thought away. How ridiculous.

"You know, you could go sit with her."

Ignoring Frank, I keep my eyes glued to the two people at the table in the back of the bar.

"I'm Adara," she smiles. "I haven't been coming here for long, but I usually hang out in the back, so you probably haven't seen me before."

Keith scoots his chair a bit closer, gesturing around the bar and then to the stage. "Yeah, I can't see well up there with the spotlights anyway to be honest. Anyway, I have to get back and play the last set. Do you plan to stay long? Maybe we can grab a drink after."

Frustrated, I move toward my office door and lean back against the wall, keeping my eyes trained on her.

"Yeah, maybe." She nods with a smile, going back to her reading as Keith gets up and strolls back to the stage.

"This song is for new beginnings," he says into the mic.

I cross my arms over my chest, my fingers digging into my skin as I watch him stare at the back of Adara's head. My wolf wants to snap his head off for looking at her like that, for talking to her about a drink like it could be some kind of date. Like she could be his. But she isn't. She's *mine*.

"Relax, boss," Frank says, sliding up beside me. "He's playing his usual set he does every night. Trying to burn holes into his guitar from here isn't going to help anything."

Still glaring at Keith, I grumble under my breath, "Get back to work, Frank. I didn't ask for your advice or your company."

He laughs. "Well, ain't that the truth. Because if you'd asked for my advice, I would've told you to stop being a gods damn fool before you lose your chance forever." He walks back to the bar, relieving Aramin to return to her tables.

Another thirty minutes passes excruciatingly slowly, and Adara slowly stops turning the pages on the book before her. She rubs her face with one hand and yawns as the band plays their last song for the night.

"You should go home," I say, as I reach her table, unable to keep myself away from her any longer.

She ignores me, flipping another page and attempting to read.

I put my hand over the paper. "Go home. You're exhausted."

Lifting her gaze to mine, her violet eyes are rimmed in silver and bore holes straight to my soul. "Is that an order from you as my alpha or my boss?"

"Both," I say slowly, matching her anger.

She rolls her eyes and returns to her reading. "I'm not finished with this text yet."

"You're practically falling asleep at the table. Leave. I won't ask you again." My hand curls into a fist on the book, ripping the page from the binding.

She snatches it out of my grasp, holding the closed book to her chest. "You haven't asked me a single thing, Gideon, and I'm not leaving." Pressing her mouth into a firm line, she inhales through her nose, holding eye contact despite me using alpha influence. Sweat beads on her forehead.

Then, my phone buzzes in my pocket.

Growling, I tear it out and glance at the screen.

Darrold: Jaz is missing.

Looking at the bar, I notice concern written over Frank's face and stand back from the table. "Go home, Adara. And no, I'm not asking. That's an immediate order." I ignore the fire burning in her eyes as I make my way to the bar, waving my phone in the air as

I walk outside to my truck. Climbing into the cab, I race over to Darrold's house.

Empty streets coated in the darkness of night allow me to reach his house in under ten minutes, and I notice Madrona's car in the drive already. Sighing, I step from the cab and walk to the front door, letting myself in. Their voices float down the hall, and I follow the sound to find them seated at the kitchen table. Madrona has her long fingers threaded into her gray-streaked black hair as she stares down at the table in front of her.

Madrona has been the busiest pack mom since I became the alpha centuries ago. When I met her, she'd taken me in immediately—as part of her nature is to take in strays. I wasn't a child then, but I was a new werewolf with nowhere to go and could only see a future of bloodshed before me. Blood and revenge. In a way, she became the pack mother I'd needed to see clearly through the pain, and it's how I know she's the best home for Jaz right now.

Darrold stands quickly. "Disantollo, thank you for coming so fast."

"Details. Now." I stay in the doorway of the kitchen, leaning my shoulder against the frame.

"She was supposed to come home after school," Madrona starts, wiping a tear from her cheek. "She texted me after to say she had a training session instead. I didn't think anything of it, really. She always talks about asking for more sessions to get a stronger hold of her wolf."

I glance over at Darrold, who clears his throat. "I never scheduled training with her today, though, and when she never came home and stopped returning texts, Madrona came here."

"So, she's been missing for..." I look at the clock, noting the time is well past midnight, "ten hours or more?"

Madrona nods, burying her face in her hands. "I've never lost one of my pups before. We have to find her." Her voice breaks, the scent of saltwater filling the air with her tears.

I move forward to rest my hand on her shoulder, my heart squeezing in my chest. "Tell me where you've looked already. You won't lose a pup on my watch, Maddie."

She raises her face to mine, cheeks wet with tears, and nods. Letting out a shaky breath, she lists various places across town—school, home, Jaz's best friend's house, the soccer fields, Jaz's old house.

Standing back, I run a hand through my hair. Sawyer's girl. A spitfire, just as her mom Bella was, and a part of me isn't surprised in the least that she already had her first shift—it usually comes out sooner after a traumatic experience, like when your dad beats the shit out of you and your mom on a regular basis and then your mom kills herself shortly after getting to a safe place.

I walk out the door without a word, knowing exactly where I'm going first and that if I could kill Sawyer over again for all the pain he's still putting his little girl through beyond the grave, I wouldn't even blink.

Fog seeps between the thick trunks of the forest. It doesn't take long for me to reach the clearing, my wolf form allowing me to see better at night despite the fog. The clearing is hidden in the woods, one that Bella had shown me once, when she was pregnant and filled with hope. I should've seen it then—the bruising hidden beneath her fur is only part of my excuse, but the pain in her eyes... Clenching my jaw, I chase the sound of a pup yipping, her voice breaking with each attempt at howling.

Slowly, I move through the brush at the tree line and find the small brown wolf pawing at the dirt floor, surrounded by a sea of pink and purple flowers. I walk over, standing beside her until she slumps to the ground with a small huff.

"*Go away,*" her small voice says.

"Oh, so you don't want to hear my stories? How much your mother loved these lady slippers? Or how she named you after her favorite flowers?"

She lifts her head to look at me, her eyes reminding me of Bella's on the night I found her here. *"She what?"*

I use my paw to nudge her snout. *"Your name, Jazelle, came from her favorite flowers. The Clematis Giselles are beautiful and shaped as stars. She always said you were her north star, the brightest one in the darkest times to show her the way."*

"So much for that. She still left me." Tears roll down her cheeks, soaking into her fur, and I lay down beside her and set my snout on top of hers.

"She loved you more than you could ever imagine, little star. But she carried her own pain too. Come on. It's late. Let's get you home."

"No," she pulls away, looking down at her paws.

I swallow back the frustration at the second girl tonight not following orders.

"Can we stay a little longer, Gideon?" She looks up at me through her lashes, fresh tears swimming in her eyes. *"Please?"* she whispers.

With a sigh, I nod and look up at the moon. *"Fine, but only because your howl is pathetic. We need to work on that."*

A small giggle echoes in my head, and I hide the smile tugging at my lips.

CHAPTER THIRTEEN
Adara

"FRANK, PLEASE," I BEG, FOLLOWING HIM ALONG the bar and tugging on his sleeve.

He sighs. "It's not a good idea."

"Why? Because Gideon will get angry? He's always angry over something." I cross my arms over my chest, refusing to go home as ordered. "I'm going to fall asleep reading any more of that book, and I could really use the extra cash."

Frank sighs, and his shoulders slump slightly.

"It's just one night. Please? I promise I won't mess it up, and you know you could use the help since Aramin left." I place my hand on his sleeve, putting on my best puppy dog eyes to plead with him. If I could wait tables now that Aramin is gone for the night, then I could get that much closer to my tuition goal for Jules. Glancing over at the door, I wonder again why she left so suddenly. Is she sick? Do werewolves even get sick like humans do? Even witches catch illnesses, but I never thought wolves did.

Frank scans the crowd again, then scratches his beard. "Fine, but if Gideon comes back, it was not my idea."

Laughing, I wrap my arms around him before grabbing the notepad and pen off the counter and walking over to the nearest table. It's easy to feel comfortable around Frank, and I'm grateful for that. "Hey, how's it going?" I smile at the two couples seated at the table, shoving down my nerves and taking their order. I bring back four beers and two orders of fries, setting them on the table before moving on to the next one.

I make sure to check on the tables Aramin left behind, one with the blonde and her friends that had been outside when I got here.

"Is everything okay? Can I get you anything else?" I'm grateful for the times I've watched Aramin wait on tables, though I don't plan to plop myself into anyone's lap like she frequently does.

Mila smiles. "No, we're all good here, thanks!"

Her friend Cali laughs. "Yeah, if we need anything, we have our own personal waitress who is more than eager to ask the bartender for drinks."

Mila blushes, punching her friend on the arm. "Hey! Shut up!"

The other two laugh harder, taunting Mila as her whole face turns red. I glance past them to Frank, seeing him smiling coyly as he winks at her. I laugh to myself, feeling happy, light on my feet, and find that waiting tables is one of the best things I've done in a while. It's easy to juggle tables like I would cleaning tasks at home, but here I don't have Monique looking over my shoulder... or Gideon staring at me from across the room, making my wolf pace inside me as she itches to feel his touch. Thinking that makes me wonder when I started to feel this comfortable—this free—around the wolves.

I shake my head to clear the thoughts from my mind and turn to walk to the next table, noting that it's Keith and the rest of the band. He was sweet when he came over to talk to me earlier, curious about the girl reading a book in a crowded bar, and his quick wit had me laughing effortlessly. I almost wish I felt any ounce of attraction for him because he would be the perfect boyfriend... for someone who wasn't a witch.

For someone who didn't already have a mate.

Blowing out a breath—and trying to blow out every bit of my anxiousness at the memory of being mated with it—I plaster a smile on my face. "Great set tonight, guys. Can I get you anything from the bar?"

"New beginnings tonight, huh, bro?" the drummer nudges Keith in the ribs, and the rest of the table laughs as Keith blushes.

"Knock it off, Aaron." Keith shoves the young drummer, looking over his shoulder at me. "Five beers, nachos, and fries, Adara. Thanks."

"You got it." I shove my notepad in my back pocket and turn to go back to the bar to talk to Frank when an arm snakes around my waist, spinning me back to the table.

"Woah, woah. Aramin always warms my lap up before she takes off."

I stumble back and land in the drummer's lap, his breath hot on my cheek. His clammy hand on my waist feels hot through my shirt and makes my skin crawl. I put both hands on his chest, pushing myself off him. "Sorry, wrong waitress."

I can hear him laughing as I walk quickly to the bar, filled with customers vying for Frank's attention. I don't know if he saw what happened, or if I should even bother telling him. Maybe this is just normal behavior, especially for Aramin's regulars. I pour the beers and return to the table, keeping my distance from Aaron, though his hungry gaze follows my every move.

"The food'll be right out." I exchange another smile with Keith and step back toward the other tables when Aaron laughs.

"Aramin was banging the alpha too, but she was never such a prude about it."

Heat flames my cheeks as images of Aramin wrapped in Gideon's arms flash in my mind. I press my lips into a tight smile and flutter my lashes at him. "Is prude the new term for a girl with standards?"

Aaron's eyes flash, and I glance at Keith next to me, who laughs with the rest of the table. "Damn, bro, she got you there," Keith says.

I walk away, jealousy flaming my insides as I try to take deep breaths to keep my wolf at bay. I don't know why I'm so surprised he's had other women before me... I mean, before we met. Gods damn it. I *knew* he'd been with other women. How could he not when he's as old as he is? But why do I care so much? It shouldn't feel like knives carving out my insides at the thought of him touching anyone but me.

I walk back to Frank to grab the food and set it on the band's table before going to check on the rest of the crowd, trying to catch my breath.

"Everything alright?" Frank asks, as I come back to gather another round of beers.

"Yeah," I say with a sigh. "Just some rowdy regulars, I guess."

His eyes flick behind me to the band's table, his brow raising slightly. His gaze comes back to me briefly before looking down the length of the crowded bar. "If you run into trouble, you let me know."

I nod, feeling suddenly shy for relying on Frank to fight my battles. It's just some drunk jerk. I should be able to handle myself instead of bothering everyone else. Plus, I won't be accepted into the pack if everyone hates me, for cheating at cards and then causing fights in the bar—not that I want the pack to accept me in the first place. Sighing, I drop the beers off at the various tables and move back to the bar, waiting in the corner for a few minutes with a glass of water.

Aaron drains his beer, then another and a third before he raises his hand. I groan inwardly, knowing nothing he wants could be good. Maybe I should've stayed in the office. Or I should've just gone home. But the thought of being alone with Gideon is just as frustrating as the idea of following one of his orders. Is it really that hard for him to just *ask*?

Putting on my best fake smile, I walk around the table to the far side. "Can I get you guys some refills?"

"Actually," Aaron says, rising from his chair and stepping around the table toward me, "I was hoping for a dance."

"Oh, no. Thanks. I'm all set. Still working." I raise a hand and wave it around the bar, glancing anxiously at Keith, who smiles apologetically. I step back as Aaron gets closer, moving around the table with my back to the bar. A part of me hopes that Frank will notice, but this table is too far from the bar for him to see us through the constant sea of people surrounding the bar top.

"One dance won't be too much trouble." He smirks, grabbing my wrist and tugging me toward him. I crash against his chest, my free hand bracing me against him as the sharp smell of beer and cigarettes fills my nose. He pulls me toward the dancefloor, the steady beat of the song playing over the speakers matches my racing heart, and I try to pull out of his grasp. But he's too strong—my wolf whimpers, and my skin turns hot.

"I really need—"

Aaron breaks through the crowd to the open dance area of the bar, pulling me forward and flicking his wrist to pull me in. He wraps an arm around my waist, pinning me tightly to him, his nails digging into my hip. "You're not turning me down, right?" he says darkly.

My stomach sinks, and my heart races. I move to step back, but his grip tightens, his nails lengthening into wolf claws and tearing through my leggings. I squeeze my eyes shut, biting the inside of my cheek as his nails scratch my skin. "I really need to be getting back to my tables. I..."

"Because if you're turning me down, then we must have a problem," he whispers against my hair, as I flinch away from his hot breath, nausea rolling through me.

I'm so stupid to think I could do this—be a wolf in their pack, in their territory, and come out unscathed. I should've known better. I should've trusted everything my coven ever told me about their kind. Their cruelty. Their mistreatment of women. Their—

Aaron's claws rip through my leggings as a hand wraps around my stomach from behind and pulls me back. Tears prick at my eyes as relief floods through me, cedarwood and caramel surrounding me like a favorite sweater.

"What do you think you're doing, Kilch?" Gideon's voice travels easily throughout the now quiet bar. Someone must've turned the stereo off, and the crowd around us is eerily silent.

I wrap my arms around myself as he lets go, backing Aaron up against the wall as he stalks toward him.

"What's the matter? No big talk tonight?" Gideon stands so close to Aaron that their faces are only inches apart. "Is there a *problem*?"

Aaron's Adam's apple bobs. "I-I was just dancing with her. Sh-she kept turning me down. She..." His eyes snap over Gideon's shoulder to land on me, and it's like a thousand spiders crawl over my body. Anger bursts through his eyes. "She was being a prude ass bitch, Disantollo. I was just showing her some hospitality."

Gideon's hand slams against the wall beside Aaron's head, snapping his attention back to him. "Is that your job?" he asks, still not raising his voice.

"W-what?" Sweat gathers on Aaron's forehead, and he shrinks back against the wall.

"Is that," Gideon says, slowly enunciating each word, "your job?"

"I..."

"Here, I'll help. No, it is not your job, drummer boy." With nails lengthened into claws, Gideon fists Aaron's shirt and drags him past me to the door. He kicks it open and throws the drummer outside.

I swallow past the lump in my throat and follow him, along with most of the bar, including the rest of the band. Aaron lands hard on the pavement, crying out as his shoulder pops out of socket, the cracking sound echoing around the still night air.

"You are the drummer of the band I hired to play here. *That* is your job." Gideon stalks over to him, towering over the trembling man on the ground clutching at his limp arm. He reaches down and grabs Aaron's shirt, ignoring the yelps of pain as he lifts his face close. "You will never lay a hand on her again. You won't even *breathe her name* or look at her."

Aaron nods frantically. "Y-yes, s-s-sir."

"You won't do those things because you're banned." Gideon throws him to the ground, and Aaron screams, hitting his injured arm on the pavement again. "Your whole band is banned from this bar." Gideon turns to face the crowd, his eyes landing on each member of the rock band. "Get out! And take your trash with you." He throws his boot into Aaron's ribs, the cracking of bones mixing with the sound of Aaron's screams.

I press a hand to my mouth, shaking at the calm display of violence. How is he so calm when he's being so cruel to his own pack? For what? Me? The powerless witch who can't even control her wolf. Isn't that what he said?

If I were to ever cross him, I wouldn't survive. He really will kill me if he thinks I tell my coven—any coven—anything about him or his pack.

And he already does. He said as much the other night.

I back up slowly, trying to control my ragged, panting breaths and calm my heart as it tries to beat out of my chest. It pounds against my ribcage, and I bite down hard on my lower lip to keep from crying. Blood pools in my mouth, and I jump when I step on a twig at the forest's edge.

Gideon's eyes snap over to mine. The rage behind the gray storm clouds of his eyes looks like a hurricane swirling in their depths and dims only slightly when his gaze finds mine. His black hair falls in waves across his face as he takes a step toward me.

A scream tears from my throat, and I whirl around, taking off into the woods, not caring about whatever direction I'm heading in. One thought rings in my head—I have to get as far from this hell as possible.

CHAPTER FOURTEEN
Gideon

THE SHARP TANG OF FEAR SEEPS INTO THE AIR, and my gaze finds Adara's. Panic is written across her features, and she screams when we make eye contact, taking off into the forest behind her. Cursing under my breath, I run after her. I strip my shirt off, loosing my wolf as I exit the easily parted crowd outside the bar.

"*Adara!*"

Her stumbling footsteps echo in the woods before me, snapping twigs and crunching leaves in a frenzy. A small yelp of pain is followed by the metallic scent of blood, and I push myself faster.

How could I have been so stupid? Of course she would panic at the sight of me dealing punishment after everything those damn witches taught her. Even if it was only to defend and protect her.

No. I was stupid long before then—to think that this could ever work between us. This arrangement was doomed from the start. From the day I chose to bite this witch instead of kill her like I should have done from the start.

Rathmann's smug face flashes in my mind along with the memory of his warning. *"If you don't clean up this mess, we'll be happy to do it for you."*

Turn around! my wolf says, annoyed that I let my anger blind me.

Skidding to a stop, I listen for a moment, hearing Adara's panting breaths and sniffling nearby. "Mia fiamma, *why are you hiding?*" I make my way slowly around a large tree trunk, finding her curled into a ball against the base. Keeping a few feet between us, I move one step closer, and my blood runs cold when she screams.

"You were going to kill him," she says. Her violet eyes are wild, silver lacing their edges. "And you'll kill me too. I—"

I pause, not wanting to move any closer and push her away, but every inch of me is begging to hold her. *"I wasn't going to kill that idiot. And why would I kill you? I have no reason to hurt you."*

"I know you will! You already think I told the council about everything, and I cheated in the bar. Why wouldn't you kill me?" She buries her face in her hands, sobs wracking through her. "You have to be toying with me, setting me up for something bigger—some punishment waiting for me... Gods, she was right. I was never destined for anything. I-I..."

"Adara..." I inch closer to her.

She shrinks back. "Don't touch me! I'll... I'll go home, and I'll get rid of my wolf, a-and... I'll never bother you again, okay?" She scoots back against the tree, scraping her hands on the rocks littering the forest floor. With another scream, she throws her head back, her body bending and morphing into her wolf just as she faints and crumples to the ground.

Something in me snaps, my chest aching, and I clench my jaw to keep the howl inside from tearing through me.

I press my snout to hers briefly before stepping back and shifting back into my human form. "Kaylus," I call.

I wait a moment for the raven to fly down from the branches, circling and cawing above me before landing on the forest floor beside his witch.

With a sigh, I step back. "Get her home. Her clothes are shredded."

The raven tilts his head, then brushes his beak against her snout. I wish I knew what he was saying, but only a witch is able to talk with her own familiar.

"I didn't hurt her, if that's what you're wondering. She... ran into some trouble at the bar, and when I stepped in to handle my rowdy pack idiot, I..." Another sigh escapes me. "I don't have to explain myself to some bird. She hyperventilated and passed out. She'll wake up in a minute. Get her home." I glare down at the bird. "Safely."

He caws in response.

Turning, I shift back to wolf form and melt back into the darkened forest, aiming for the lake.

BITTEN WITCH

Laying on the grassy bank after swimming in the freezing lake, I stare up at the night sky. "It's all your fault, you know."

My fault? my wolf asks, incredulous.

"Yes," I snap. "You made it sound so easy. She's my mate. I shouldn't be such an ass. Make it work. *Play nice.*"

I never said play nice. I also don't see how any of this is my fault. She is *our mate, you fool.*

I scoff. "She's a witch. A powerless witch who can't control her wolf. What am I supposed to do with that?"

Train her, for gods' sake. You've shut me up for centuries only to become this dumb? Gideon Disantollo, you're losing your touch.

Growling, I glare at the starry sky. "You mangy bastard. I'll shut you up again after all this."

You can't blame me because you grew hopeful. Just like you can't blame me for losing Ella and Grace.

"Shut up," I snarl, lumbering to my feet and hurling the nearest thing I can find—a rock the size of my palm. I launch it at the woods, and my brows furrow at the sound of a sharp *ouch.*

"What the hell, Dee? You hit me with that." Aramin moves through the tree line, naked with her long red hair falling over her shoulders.

"What're you doing here?" I arch a brow at her, then lay back down on the grass.

She huffs. "Checking on you, obviously. Someone had to. You've been gone for ages after you beat Aaron and banned the whole crew. What's up with that?"

"It's none of your business." I keep my eyes trained on the sky above, my mind drifting to the memory of Aaron's arms wrapped around Adara, the way her eyes were pinched shut and her body was tense. I could beat the hell out of him again for it.

And prove to her you're every bit the monster she thinks you are.

"And she'd be right," I mutter.

"What?" Aramin looks over at me as she sits down.

"What do you want, Aramin?" I sigh, looking over at her. "Let's not pretend you're here out of the goodness of your heart."

She scowls at me for a moment before her chest deflates. "I left for five minutes and came back to hear that you freaked out all because of some new girl. I've seen her around. In your office." She shrugs, picking at the blades of grass by her thigh. "Is she your... you know?"

"Aramin—"

"I'm just... I still love you. I think—I think we could really work out. If we tried this time. You know? I-I want to be with you, Dee."

A loud laugh escapes me. "We were never together. We slept together once, with clear boundaries that it was a one time deal. Don't push your delusional expectations onto me."

Standing, I leave her sitting on the grassy bank and shift into my wolf and run back to the bar. Guilt tugs at my gut for leaving her there, but everything I said was true. At every chance, she's tried to lay claims to me—to the alpha's status, but power has always been her only priority, something that became clear after that mistake of a night.

A week has passed with Adara skipping every shift. Hell, she could come back demanding to be a waitress again, and I'd let her. I miss her scent, like the forest on a winter night. I miss how easily her wolf responded to my own, the way her hair fell across her face. I miss her eyes—so deeply purple they looked almost navy in the dimness of the bar.

My wolf laughs, the sound grating on my nerves, and I shove the thoughts of her from my mind, though the shame of showing her my true nature and scaring her away lingers like a tender scar.

A knock sounds on my office door, and I peer up to see Aramin pushing it open. "Dee?" She sways her hips as she walks into the room and shuts the door behind her.

Irritation bubbles up inside me. "What?"

Annoyance flits across her face, and she stands with one hand on her hip. "I have customers asking what band'll be playing tonight since you went psycho on the last one."

Groaning, I lean my head back against the chair. I don't regret banning Aaron and his stupid group, especially when no one bothered to help Adara when she clearly didn't want to be touched. My hands grip the arms of my chair, the wood squeaking beneath my fingers.

Aramin walks over and rests her hand on top of mine. "She's just some dumb new wolf, Dee. I don't understand why you're so uptight about it."

I shrug her hand off mine and push back from my desk. "Play the stereo until I find a new band. Let anyone who asks know that there's an opening."

She grabs my arm when I brush past her toward the door. "Come on, how long are you going to be mad at me?" Stepping into me, she brushes her chest against mine, dragging one finger down my cheek. "Can't I make it up to you?"

Grabbing her wrists, I push her back. "I'm not mad at you. I just don't care to have you draped over me constantly, acting like you'll ever be my mate."

"Is that what she is—your mate? That girl who couldn't even be proud of you standing up for her when she was too weak to do it herself?" She scoffs, throwing her hands in the air. "You're tossing me aside for *her*?"

Curling my hands into fists, I stride toward my door and throw it open, gesturing for her to leave.

She laughs dryly, no trace of humor found on her face. "Everyone knows she cheated at cards for days, and now this? You're losing your touch." Walking out of the office, she pauses to pat my cheek before walking back out to the bar filled with tables and plopping down onto the lap of the nearest guy.

I slam the door shut, letting the wood rattle the hinges, the frame splintering slightly.

"Well, she sure is pleasant."

I look up to find Rathmann at the window, walking to my desk and settling down onto a chair.

"I take it you didn't fix that little problem then." He rests an ankle over his knee, draping his naked form across the chair lazily, but the look in his eyes is predatory. "I'll let the council know. There's really only one way to set the balance back and protect our kind—"

"No." I walk over and pour myself a glass of whiskey, downing half before harshly setting it back on the desk. I have half a mind to toss him a spare pair of sweatpants again, but I don't want him to think it's another invitation to stay longer than necessary. "It's been dealt with."

Rathmann's brows raise, and a playful smile breaks across his face. "Really? Well, what a surprising turn of events. From the way that one talked," he gestures over his shoulder at the door, "I was beginning to think you actually mated with the witch." He throws his head back and laughs.

I smile tightly. "If there's nothing else?"

He chuckles one last time, moving closer to the window. "No, not today, Disantollo." Waving over his shoulder, he launches out the window—that I need to start locking—and shifts into his wolf, tongue lolling out of his mouth as he looks back at me before taking off into the woods.

The minute he's out of sight, I shut the window and throw the rocks glass across the room, watching the glass shatter against the door and the shards rain down.

CHAPTER FIFTEEN
Adara

GIDEON LOOMS OVER ME AS I LAY SPRAWLED ON the floor of the bar. I scramble back, trying to create as much distance between us as possible. His eyes glow silver in the darkness, and his bones creak and pop as he starts to shift, a deep growl rumbling in his chest.

"Stop, please! I didn't tell them anything!" I move back, losing my balance and smacking my elbow on the hard floor. Moaning, I try to cradle it to my chest. I want to move, watching as Gideon keeps moving toward me, but I'm frozen.

"You think you can learn all our secrets and sell us out like cattle, little witch? You think you're better than us?" His voice echoes around me, hatred and rage burning in his eyes. He lunges for me, and I scream as his hand wraps around my throat. "You're the worst of us," he whispers in my ear. "A traitor to both kinds. You have no family. You're *nothing*."

I try to tear his fingers off, sobbing as his fangs pierce my neck—

"*Addy!*" Kaylus's voice breaks through the fog, and I bolt upright in bed, my sheets sticking to my sweat drenched body.

Panting, I press my hand over my chest, my heart beating wildly against my palm. I glance at the time—just after midnight.

It's been a week since I watched Gideon calmly beat a member of his own pack, and the guilt has been eating at me. Guilt for not stopping it, for almost wanting it to happen when Aaron never took no for an answer, and fueled more when I think of every girl he's pushed himself onto. But then shame overshadows those feelings because I *am* a traitor, trying to control my wolf and learning about the pack, believing Gideon and Frank over my coven.

Smoothing my damp hair back from my face, I get out of bed and grab my sweatshirt, tugging it on and slipping on my boots. I climb out the window as Kaylus circles above me and make my way into the woods, the gentle breeze causing goosebumps to spread over my skin.

"Are you ever going to stop looking for this wishing well?" Kaylus asks, impatient.

"No," I huff. "I have to get rid of my wolf. This is the only way I know how." A noose of sadness cinches around my heart, and I try to brush it off.

"You could go back to training."

I stop walking and stare up at the raven. "Go back? To do what, die? He'll kill me, Kaylus!"

He caws once before flying ahead. *"If he was going to kill you, you'd already be dead. Instead, he protected you when you refused to stand up for yourself."*

Scowling at the bird, I stomp my way through the woods and into Lockwood Forest. The night darkens when I break through the thicket of trees, and the air around me feels stale. Silence seeps in, swirling around my shoulders like silk, and I shiver.

I've come out here every night this week trying to find the well my grandmother spoke of, but every time I feel myself get close, the forest seems to shift. The paths move, the trees close in. A scent of dark magic—ashy and blackened—curls around me every time, then transports me back home. I wake up in the morning in my bed, wearing the same clothes as the night before with twigs in my hair.

My wolf whimpers in my head, and I shake it, trying to shut her up. She's become louder since I left—constantly pushing me to Gideon and the Silver Lycans bar. She drags up memories of him—his wolf howling at the moon, his lips and body pressed against mine in the lake, the way his curls fall across his eyes.

Sighing, I glower at the leaves beneath my boots, knowing she's doing it again. "I'm not going back to that monster," I mumble, panic lacing through me when I remember the calmness surrounding him when he completely lost it on Aaron.

But panic is quickly replaced with anger.

Why didn't Keith stop him? Why didn't he help me? *No one* helped me. I didn't even help myself. Why can't I just stand up for myself for once? The only one

I've ever been able to do that with is Gideon, and the fact only serves to infuriate me.

Because he's the one I've felt true comfort with.

Because he's the one I've been able to be myself around. Not the powerless witch. Not the maid of the house. Not the protective big sister.

Just *me*.

"You've been moping for days, Addy." Kaylus circles above me as I stumble over the loose rocks and stray roots covering the ground. *"And I think you know why as well as I do."*

"I don't know what you're talking about," I mutter, refusing to admit that he's right. Gideon swallows my every waking thought, and whether it's my wolf's doing or my own—I miss him and his insufferable attitude.

Kaylus caws above me, then slowly drifts down and lands on my shoulder.

"Do you really think he was just protecting me?" I ask quietly, remembering his arm wrapping around my waist and pulling me out of Aaron's grasp, the relief that washed over me at being safe and knowing it was Gideon behind me.

"Is there any other explanation for why you're still alive and that jerk is banned for life from his own pack bar?" He nuzzles his beak into my cheek for a moment.

Letting the question hang in the air, I try to focus on the wishing well and the path before me. Tonight, I decided to try a different route, hoping that the magic swirling in the forest isn't the same from every direction.

But when my boots become heavy and the trees no longer creak and sway in the breeze, my stomach sinks.

"Not again," I groan, as my wolf whines.

The dirt path shifts beneath my feet, and I stumble to the side, falling into the trunk of a maple tree and scraping both palms on the rough bark. Ash coats my tongue, and I gag at the taste, the scent of Palo Santo swirling thickly in the air around me. Kaylus's claws dig deeper into my shoulder, and the trees blur together in a cyclone of colors.

The last thing I see is a woman, maybe a few years older than me, standing in a clearing just up ahead with a blood red cloak hanging about her shoulders. The hood is drawn up, blanketing her face in shadows, but unmistakable eyes stare back at me—silver.

She lifts a hand, holding out two fingers, and blackness swallows me.

Sunlight pours through my window, and the sound of something hitting the glass pane wakes me up.

Groggy, I rub a hand over my face and yawn, then sit up and see Kaylus sitting outside, perched on the sill of my window. I get up to let him inside, and the night before slowly seeps back into my memory.

"Damn it, it happened again." I run a hand through my hair, pulling out stray leaves and sticks before gathering it into a ponytail. Groaning, I rush downstairs to start breakfast and coffee. As I go to throw yesterday's coffee grounds into the trash, a white envelope catches my eye.

Juliana Morrow.

Academy of Witches.

My fingers reach in to grab it and tear it open, scanning the contents quickly. Monique must have thrown this away—it's dated three days ago.

"Final notice that tuition is due in full by January first for the following autumn semester enrollment."

Chewing on my lower lip, I scan the rest of the document. A door creaks, and I stuff it into my back pocket just as Monique walks into the kitchen.

"What are you doing just standing there by the garbage, Adara? You're letting the toast burn. Honestly." Sighing, she shakes her head at me and moves to sit down at the table. Being the weekend, she doesn't have to go into work, though she normally ends up going in by lunch regardless.

"Sorry, Mother," I mumble.

"Stop mumbling. You know how much I hate when you mumble. Have you even woken your sister up yet, or were you planning to eat without her?"

Fixing a cup of coffee, I bring the mug to the table and set it before her. "I was trying to let her rest until it was ready."

"If you let her rest too long, then it'll be cold when she gets down here." She takes a sip of the coffee and scowls down into the mug before placing it on the table. "One sugar, not three."

Turning to the stairs, I take a deep breath. "It was only one sugar, Mom. I'll wake Jules up now, then finish breakfast."

She sighs loudly from behind me while I head upstairs.

After breakfast, Monique heads into her office to study with Jules while I clean and check off each task from her daily list of chores. As much as I hate scrubbing the baseboards, I don't envy Jules for being stuck in that room all morning going over the coven rules, witches, and practices.

It's barely lunch by the time they come out, Monique announcing that she's leaving for the office for the rest of the day.

"What's next? I can help!" Jules says once she's backed down the driveway and on her way to the city.

I walk to the counter and glance at the list. "Let's see. You could wash the dishes, and I'll vacuum.

Then, I can tackle the yard when you do the bathrooms."

Jules claps her hands together. "Alright, let's do this!" She giggles and dances over to the speakers, turning on the radio before diving into the dishes.

The rest of the day passes by quickly, and it isn't until dinner is done and on the table that we realize Monique is late for the first time in years.

"Did she call?" Jules asks, knowing we don't have a phone to text her. One of the many *isolating* rules of the house—no cell phones unless you're Monique.

I shake my head and shrug. "Well, let's eat, and I'll put a plate for her in the fridge."

She chews on her lip for a moment, glancing nervously at the door. "O-okay..."

Halfway through dinner, the house phone rings. Jules jumps up to grab it from the counter.

"Mama? Okay... yes, I studied... The house is clean... No, really. It is... O-okay, I'll see you tomorrow... Bye, Mama." She hangs up and turns to me. "Um, she said she had to go view a property for work and didn't expect it to take this long so she'll be home tomorrow."

I shove a piece of bread into my mouth and smile. "Sweet. Movie night!"

Jules's face turns from anxious to excited. "Really? With popcorn?"

"Heck yeah! Popcorn *and* sundaes!" I laugh when she ditches the rest of dinner to raid the freezer, finding the small ice cream cups hidden in the back.

BITTEN WITCH

Monique never lets us stay up late, let alone watch TV for non-educational purposes or eat junk food. Chloe mentioned a couple of properties being far drives, but she thought Monique would send *her* to look at them, not go herself. Whatever, though, I'll happily take advantage of the rare peaceful night.

"Jules," I whisper, crossing into her room from the hall. "Will you be okay if I go for a walk?"

She smiles sleepily. "Yeah, for a *walk*. I hope you find whatever used to make you happy out there, Addy."

Confused, I sit down on her bed, brushing her blonde hair off her face. "What're you talking about?"

"You used to be happy. I don't know what happened, but last week, you seemed sadder than before. Go," she yawns, "find your happy, big sis."

She rolls over and snuggles down into her blankets, and my heart breaks. She cooked popcorn using a spell tonight, gathering enough heat to not burn it but pop every kernel perfectly. She *deserves* to go to the academy.

Squaring my shoulders, I slowly back out of her room and rush down the stairs and out to the woods toward Silver Lycans. My wolf paces in my chest, excited to get to the bar and see Gideon, though I keep reminding her—and myself—that we aren't going to see him. We're going for Jules.

I swallow my anxiety as I pull open the bar door and step inside. Gideon sits at a table near the stage, lounging back on the chair while a new band plays a song. His eyes cut over to mine when the door clicks shut behind me, and my stomach somersaults.

Ignoring the band, he stands and walks over to me, grabbing both my hands in his. The gesture is so sweet and intimate that my cheeks flame.

"You're back," he says, his gray eyes searching mine.

I step back, pulling my hands from his. "I-I didn't say anything. I stayed quiet," I whisper. "I just wanted to come back and ask to, um, wait tables for the tips."

He clears his throat, shoving his hands into his jeans pockets. "Actually, if you don't mind another job, I could use your help."

"Oh. I—"

"I can pay you the same as you made the other night in tips, plus the usual pay." He scans the bar, and I follow his gaze, noticing it isn't as crowded in here as it normally is. "You'll make more that way."

I nod slowly and follow him back to the table near the stage where a band is playing, taking a seat on the chair opposite him.

"I have to hire a new band. It's part of the whole attraction," he says, waving his hand around at the bar. "But I don't listen to music anymore, so I need someone to tell me what sounds good and what people would actually like."

I scrunch my brows together. "You can't tell what sounds good?"

A small smile tugs at one side of his mouth. "I guess that isn't necessarily true. I can point out what sucks pretty easily, like these fools."

A surprised laugh escapes me, and I cover my mouth with one hand.

"Next band," he calls, dismissing the punk rock cover band from the stage.

After a few bands take the stage, Gideon announces that we're taking a ten minute break. He walks over to the bar to talk to Frank, and Aramin comes over to drop a soda on the table before me.

"Here," she says curtly. She turns to leave, then whirls back around. "Don't feel like you're special, either. He slept with me just last night in the office. The only reason he's so interested in trash like you is because you're playing hard to get." She leans forward, her minty perfume filling my nose. "And when he tires of you as his new plaything, he'll punish you for every problem you've caused in this pack."

Raising my brows, I lean back in my seat to create some distance, fighting back the initial panic of wondering if Gideon will truly punish me. "I'm not even interested in him, so you can have him." My wolf snarls at the lie pouring out of my mouth, but right now, I'm too angry to care.

Aramin laughs, standing and flicking her red ponytail over one shoulder. "Whatever."

I glance over my shoulder at Gideon still talking with Frank, then look at the closed office door. Did he really sleep with her?

Jealousy coils in my gut, and I'm rising out of my seat, heading toward the office door, before I realize what I'm doing.

CHAPTER SIXTEEN
Gideon

FRANK GLANCES BEHIND ME AT THE DOOR. "Someone said they thought a brown wolf was stalking the bar from the woods."

"And you think it's Rathmann?" I run a hand through my hair, wondering why the council is choosing to spy on me instead of their usual harassment.

Frank shrugs. "I didn't say that, but I wouldn't put it past them." He slides a glass over to me.

Sipping the whiskey, I think it over. He accepted the fact that I'd dealt with Adara myself a bit too easily... "Send a patrol out. If it isn't Rathmann, I'd like to know what pack is doing recon on us. If it is him, I want to know what his excuse is for hiding."

He nods as I put the empty glass on the bar and turn back to the stage. I signal to the next band to start up, dreading the rest of the night listening to this garbage. We've heard three bands already tonight, and none of them have sounded anywhere close to decent.

Heading back to the table, I look around for Adara. As I take a seat, noting the full glass of soda I'd sent over for her, I flag Aramin down as she walks by. "Where is she?"

"Who?" she asks, smiling sweetly.

"Don't play dumb with me," I growl.

The smile falls off her face, and she lifts a shoulder. "I only told her not to get her hopes up. Not my fault she chose to snoop for evidence of us sleeping together last night."

I stand up, stepping close and putting my face just a breath away from hers. "I wouldn't call you sneaking into my office to try—and fail at—seducing me *sleeping together*. I wouldn't touch you if you were the last she-wolf on Earth. Do I make myself clear?"

She swallows hard and nods.

Leaning back, I raise a brow. "Good. Get back to work." I watch her walk to the next table before I look over at my office door. Fucking Aramin, forever the largest thorn in my side.

With a huff, I make my way toward the side of the bar, noting that the current band—one of the new shifters Darrold is training—isn't half bad.

I push open the door and step inside the room, shutting it loudly behind me. Adara jumps, turning around with wide eyes.

"Looking for something in particular?" I ask, scanning the office. Books are scattered around the floor, and the cot is pulled out. The notebooks and papers on my desk are strewn across it, spread out from the neat piles I'd made earlier.

Adara's eyes narrow at me, the silver swallowing up each speck of violet in her irises. "What is this? I find out you're sleeping with that waitress, and now you're married?" She throws the piece of paper at me, and it flutters to the ground at my feet.

I hold her gaze, matching her glare. "Jealous, little witch? My past is none of your concern. Aramin was a one time *mistake* from decades ago."

She laughs humorlessly. "Jealous? I'd have to care to be jealous, Gideon. And unlike your wife, I can spot a liar."

Clenching my jaw, my eyes snap down at the paper—the photo. I reach down, snatching it off the floor and brushing it off. Ella and Grace smile back at me in the photo, just days before the witches came, and the image of Ella's burnt body flickers in my mind. "Get out," I whisper. My anger rises with every second. The small tear in the corner setting my insides ablaze, my vision becoming one silvery fire for a brief moment. "Get out, Adara!"

Her brows furrow, and her lips form a tight line. "That's it? You're not even going to deny it? You kissed me! You called me your *mate!* Does she even know what kind of bastard she married? What kind of man she has for her child's father?" Her voice breaks, and she angrily swipes the tears from her cheeks. "I wish I never met you. I hate you and your godsforsaken pack!"

I tuck the photo into my back pocket and stalk toward her. "I said get out." I inject all the alpha influence I can, and her eyes widen as her feet move slowly to the door. "You have no right to be in here. Now *get out*. You don't want me asking questions about your life? About who will kill you if they know what you are? Then, don't act like you have a right to mine." I grab her upper arms and drag her to the door, flinging it open and shoving her into the bar before slamming it shut in her face.

In the dim light of the office, I reach into my pocket and take out the photo, the only memory I have, perfectly preserved by the one good witch in this world. Tears pool in my eyes as I stare down at the family in the photo—*my* family. I was so young when I met Ella, young still when we had Grace. I love them more than I can bear, even still, after all this time. My soul struggles under the weight of my grief as their deaths haunt me worse than any ghost possibly could.

509 Years Ago

"We're low on meat, my love," Ella calls from inside.

I come to stand behind her as she watches Grace toddle on the floor, Wrapping my arms around her waist from behind, I nuzzle my nose into her neck, inhaling her sweet perfume, like that of the rose petals she gathers each day for a tonic she drinks before bed.

Ella laughs, raising a hand to bury it in my hair. "Did you hear me about the meat?"

"Mmm," I say into her neck, earning another laugh. I kiss her shoulder gently. "I'll leave now while there's still daylight and find a deer. It's nearing dusk as it is."

Kissing Ella's cheek, I step around her to scoop Grace off the floor. "My sweet girl, look how big you're getting!"

She kicks her legs in the air, and a happy smile breaks across her face, dimples forming in her chubby cheeks.

I kiss them each goodbye and grab my hunting bow, leaving to go into the woods as dusk begins to settle over the forest surrounding our small home. I find my usual hunting field, settling into the cover I'd made from the times before. It isn't long before I hear rustling in the leaves around me, and I steady my bow and arrow. As the noise grows closer, I peer around the trunk of a tree, taking aim with the help of the near full moon.

I loose the arrow, watching it soar through the air at the intended flank of the deer just a few yards ahead, but another noise startles it. I curse under my breath as it runs off, and the arrow buries into a trunk not too far beyond. Hearing nothing, I move to retrieve the arrow, refusing to lose a good arrow if I can avoid it. Just as I reach to pull it out, a stick breaks behind me.

Whirling around, I nock another arrow and raise my bow, but fiery pain erupts on my calf as teeth sink deep into my flesh, grating on the bone. I scream, crumpling to the ground and grasping at my torn pants, wet with blood as the monster releases me.

The creature comes closer, and I try to get to my feet, but my leg refuses to bear any weight. I fall, landing hard on my back, and stare up into the eyes of a wolf the size of a bear. The wolf growls, every large tooth shining in the moonlight as saliva drips from its jowls.

Its ear twitches, and I grapple on the ground, looking for my sack. My fingers curl around an arrow, and I grit my teeth through the pain of the movement as I shove it into the wolf's ribs. It yelps and backs away, limping as it flees into the woods. I lay on the ground, wheezing in the cold air as I stare up at the night sky, the stars dancing in my vision before darkness consumes me.

The next morning, sunlight shines through the trees, waking me. After making my way home, Ella cleans and dresses my wounds, forcing me to rest for the remainder of the day. We stare strangely down at my leg, looking at the iridescent scars in two half circles around my calf—wounds that shouldn't have healed this quickly.

"You can't go out again, Gideon," she begs that evening. "That wolf could come back, and then what would we do? How will we survive without you?"

I can't explain the burning in my chest, the deep desire in my soul to go out into the woods. "I need to feed you, or we'll all die. My heart, please." I wipe a tear from her cheek and kiss her forehead. "I will be back by morning."

No deer come as I wait in the woods, but as the full moon rises in the sky, the burning in my chest deepens to an inferno. My skin explodes in the flames, and my body breaks and reforms.

As dawn breaks over the land, I stagger home. The horizon, that should be dark until the sun's rays touch it, blazes unnaturally before me. I push through the pain and exhaustion, my mind unable to register through the fog of my panic that the fire isn't spreading despite the kindling stacked near the house.

Breaking through the trees, I fall to my knees. My home burns brightly against the darkness, flames licking at the sky above. "Ella!" I scream, crawling forward as I get to my feet and race closer to the house.

Wood beams creak and snap within the fire, embers flying into the sky as they break and fall.

"Ella!" My fingers bury in my hair, tugging at the strands as smoke clogs my lungs and burns my eyes. "Ella!" My voice breaks, tears streaming down my face as no one answers.

So consumed by my heartache, I don't register the wolf coming to sit beside me until he speaks.

"The witches came, boy," he says.

I jump at the sound of another's voice in my mind, and the wolf laughs darkly.

"Come. They came for you, and they'll come again."

"M-my wife... my daughter, they're in there."

"They're gone. Look, there in the window."

I look through the window to see my wife, petrified eerily despite the flames, bound to a chair, her mouth hanging open in a silent scream. "Ella... Ella!" I move to rush into the house, but the wolf darts in front of me.

"It's magical flames, boy, don't be a fool."

"What are you?" I scream. "What are you talking about?"

"Not here," the wolf says, and he walks away, looking back over his shoulder as he waits for me to follow him.

I slump onto the cot, reliving the nightmare of their loss again and again. The witches burned my family alive that night, trying to capture me, just as my alpha wolf described that night, along with the rest of the details of this supernatural world I was dragged into. A sob chokes me, the memory of Grace and Ella painfully raw despite the time that's passed, carved into my soul as a permanent wound that will never heal.

My wolf burns hot in my chest, and I struggle to keep him locked inside. I refuse to chase after that witch or feel guilty for the way she left, with tear stained cheeks and a heart I shattered. I'm every bit the monster she thinks I am, and it's better for us both that she realizes it now, before my mistakes cost her her life too.

CHAPTER SEVENTEEN
Adara

SITTING AGAINST THE BRICK WALL OF THE BAR, I swipe the tears off my cheeks. He is a monster, so why do I feel so horrible leaving him like that?

"Addy?" Kaylus caws and flies down from a branch above me. *"What's wrong?"*

I sniffle, wiping my nose on my sleeve and resting my forehead on my knees as I pull them up to my chest. "He's awful. I can't go back in there."

Kaylus hops along on the gravel and rubs his beak on my thigh.

"That girl told me they slept together last night, and then I went into his office and found a photo, and it was his *wife*." Hot tears pour down my cheeks. The betrayal I feel at seeing that photo, despite its obvious age being from so long ago, is unreal. If she's a werewolf too, then she would still be alive, so where is she?

The bar door opens, clanking shut as footsteps crunch over the ground. I bury my face harder into my knees, wrapping my arms around my legs. Someone sits down beside me, resting their arm around my shoulders.

"Hey, love, you alright?" Frank asks, his deep voice soft and comforting.

"Why didn't anyone tell me Gideon was married?" I lift my face to look at him, angry with him for keeping his alpha's secrets. "You should've told me."

He sighs, his thumb rubbing my shoulder, and raises his face to the night sky. "It wasn't my place to share his past."

"And Aramin? That's his past? Because she made it sound an awful lot like she's his present," I mumble.

Frank laughs softly. "Aramin doesn't care about Gideon, love. She cares about being an alpha's wife, mated or not. She was someone he turned to for comfort once. A long time ago."

I swallow past the lump in my throat at the image of her wrapped in his arms, bile burning the back of my throat. "So, his wife... she isn't a wolf too?"

He shakes his head, and the relief flooding my mind steals my breath. "He's a hurting man, and hurt people lash out to hurt others. He only knows how to push everyone away." He squeezes my shoulders. "It isn't my place to tell you his story, but I'll tell you this. Don't trust Aramin—if you trust anyone, trust me. Gideon's wife is a part of his past—a very painful past." For a few moments, he sits there with me, Kaylus resting against my leg. "I need to get back in there, but think it over. Maybe consider why you didn't leave just now but chose to wait around instead." Then, with a sad smile, he gets up and heads back into the bar.

"*Maybe you should try to let him explain,*" Kaylus says.

I scoff, annoyed with the raven and the bartender all the same. "Right, like when I asked him about the photo and he kicked me out."

Kaylus tilts his head. "*Did you ask him or accuse him?*"

Scowling at the raven, I ignore him. I know I asked… but maybe not in the most open-minded type of way. I chew on my lip. Gods, this is frustrating to care despite not wanting to.

"*Maybe you should try asking to listen, instead of accusing him of being the monster you already think he is.*" He flaps his wings, taking off into the trees above me.

"Why are you defending him? Are you pro-wolf now?"

"*I'm pro-whatever makes you happy, Addy,*" he says softly.

Fresh tears pool in my eyes, and I take a few deep breaths to calm my emotions, getting my wolf under control to avoid a shift. She whimpers, urging me to go back into the bar and back to our mate. Sighing, I climb back to my feet and turn to go back inside.

Frank smiles at me as I walk inside, letting the door clang shut as I walk down the bar. He gestures over his shoulder at the office door, and I gulp as I reach to knock on the door. Muffled voices come from behind the wood, and I pause. I turn the handle and slowly open the door.

Gideon is curled on the cot sitting in the middle of the ruined room. More books than those I tore from the shelves litter the ground, glass shards cover the floor, and whiskey permeates the air and runs down the walls in streaks. I step into the office, moving to the cot, when a gathering of red hair flowing to the floor catches my eye.

"Get out," Gideon mutters.

A slender hand reaches up to cup his cheek. "Dee, I just want—"

"Stop." He pulls back, pushing Aramin's hand away. "Just leave. Go back to work and do your damn job for once."

"Gods, I'm just trying to comfort you!" she snaps, shoving his shoulder and getting off the cot. "All you care about is that stupid old photo." She grabs the photo from his hands and throws it to the ground.

"Go be a bitch to someone else, Aramin, or you're fired," Gideon says. He sounds defeated, sad, and my heart aches at the pain in his voice. Where is the fire and rage he showed me over this photograph?

She turns around, finding me in the doorway. "Oh, look. She came back." Aramin rolls her eyes and stomps from the office, slamming the door shut behind her.

Gideon rolls onto his back and looks at me. His cheeks glisten in the low light of the office, wet with tears, and I rush forward, kneeling at the side of the cot. "Y-you're crying," I whisper.

He laughs. "So are you."

"I've never seen you cry. I didn't even know you could cry."

His laugh deepens. "Because I'm a wolf?"

"No, because you're a real jerk." I smile, sniffling. Reaching down, I pick up the photo and brush the dirt off. Staring down at the picture in my hands, I see the same face that Gideon wears today, yet he looks like a complete stranger. The young auburn haired woman holds a bundle in her arms, wrapped in a blanket, and the man beside her—Gideon—looks so... happy. His smile could light up the night sky, the joy reaching his eyes, crinkled at the edges. The scowl I've come to expect on his face doesn't exist, and instead, love pours out of him like a beacon. My heart lodges in my throat as I hand the picture to him, realizing something horrible happened to have changed this man into who he's become. "I'm sorry."

Gideon sighs, reaching out to cup my cheek. "No, I'm sorry. I shouldn't have yelled at you like that."

I press my cheek into his palm, inhaling his scent and allowing myself to enjoy the intimacy of his touch.

"Ask me."

I open my eyes to find his, gray and as full of a pained past as a cloud is full of rain. "Ask you what?"

"Anything," he whispers, grabbing my hand and pulling me onto the cot with him.

I lick my lips, laying on the small bed and facing him. "Will you tell me about your family?"

He takes a deep breath and closes his eyes. "It was centuries ago when I became a wolf. I had a wife and a child. A daughter. Ella was everything I could've dreamed of having. Kind, selfless, and she loved me more than I deserved. I was attacked by a wolf one night while hunting, but we didn't know anything about this world of supernatural creatures back then. We were merely humans, living our lives." He pauses, brushing his fingers along my collarbone. "The next night was a full moon, similar to when you had your first shift. She begged me not to go, but the feeling, the pull of the moon on my wolf... I couldn't resist it. When I returned, my home... My home was in flames." His voice breaks, and so does my heart.

"Oh, Gideon," I whisper, my tears dripping down as his begin to form as well.

"The witches tortured my wife, tied her to a chair, and when she offered no valuable information on where I was or where they could capture me," his voice hardens and he clenches his jaw, "they killed her and my daughter in the house fire."

My chest aches, the feeling hollow and all-encompassing as he mourns for his family before me. All because witches—my family—killed his. A part of me wants to tell him that he's wrong, that it could've been some other murderer on a rampage and not witches, but I know he isn't. The covens have been obsessed with finding our own immortality like the wolves have for as long as I can remember—it's the entire reason for the animosity between us. It's detailed heavily in every history book—how the witches are desperate to find a way to become immortal, the jealousy over why the wolves were granted the gods' blessing like this and we weren't. Every spell book I've read goes over the spells my ancestors have tried to use on wolves in the past and how unsuccessful they each were—each failing with a dead werewolf and no immortality exchanged.

Bile rises in the back of my throat, and I work to swallow it down. How could I think so low of my own family—my coven? Because of one man's story and his pain? What if he shifted for the first time and killed a small town? What if it was a normal house fire that consumed his home and killed his family? He wasn't even home that night…

But, deep down, I know the truth in his words like I know the truth of my own scars. The witches can be cruel.

CHAPTER EIGHTEEN
Gideon

"I'M SO SORRY," ADARA WHISPERS. LOOKING AT her, her eyes are so filled with sorrow that it almost matches my own. "I don't understand how they could do something so horrible..."

"Don't you?" I ask, remembering the first nights I saw her. The scars that decorated her skin. The fear in her eyes. "Isn't it a witch you're so afraid of?"

She sighs. "I mean, yes, but... it's not the same."

I move my head forward, pressing my forehead to hers. "It is the same. You fear for your life, *mia fiamma*. Please, tell me who it is that hurts you."

She pulls back, her brows furrowed. "No... I trust them with my family—my sister. Not all witches are cruel and heartless murderers."

"Just as not all wolves are monsters."

Guilt shadows her features. "Right, I guess that is a fair point."

I take my thumb and rub the crease between her brows, trying not to push her, but inside, my wolf is snarling to know who hurt her, who she fears. "I won't let anyone hurt you—wolf or witch. I got my revenge for my family, and there is no one who dares to cross me again. Now, I only mourn their memory and for the pain I know they felt."

"Your revenge?" She moves away, sitting up on the edge of the cot and looking at me.

I smirk, attempting to ignore the emptiness around me at the loss of her body heat. "The Salem Witch Trials, of course."

Confused, her eyes narrow at me. "The... You participated?"

I chuckle, remembering those witches burning at the stake. "Oh, darling, I *started* them."

"You started them?" She stands, pacing the office floor.

I raise an arm to tuck it behind my head, smiling at the memory. "I did. I murdered every witch involved in the house fire that killed my family, and I led the witch trials to make sure everyone remembered the scorn of Gideon Disantollo." I shrug. "It was also the way I met the witch who gave me that photo. She was able to craft it for me from a memory, and it's my most treasured possession. See? I know not all witches are evil." My laughter dies in my throat at the look on her face—a mix between horror, hatred, and rage.

"Why would you do that?" She stops pacing to glower at me.

"Can you hear yourself? Why would I seek justice for my murdered family?"

"You had no right to kill all those witches. What about the humans that were falsely accused because of the rumors you started?"

"Falsely accused?" I shake my head, raising up onto my elbow. "No humans were falsely accused, Adara. The witches who survived crafted an amazing tale of mistreatment and murder for history. Anything to paint us wolves in the worst light."

"Us? There is no *us*, Gideon." She steps back when I reach for her, and I let my hand fall back to the cot, pushing myself into a sitting position. "You murdered so many of my ancestors."

I press my lips together, moving to my desk and pouring a glass of whiskey. "I murdered those who were murderers. It's a simple trade, and I made the world a better place once they were gone." I drain my glass, keeping my eyes on her as she stares at me, then set it on the wood desk. "And I'd kill them again if given the chance. If any were truly your ancestors, you're better off without them tainting your innocence."

"You're no better than they are," she says, storming over to me and poking a finger into my chest. "You're a murderer just as they were."

I grab her wrist, pulling her tight against me and wrapping my other arm around her waist. "I murdered those who killed for their own wants and desires. For their own coveted goals. They murdered innocents—my *child*—just to get to me when I was someone who had done nothing to them."

She scoffs, trying to pull away from me, but I tighten my hold around her, gripping her chin with one hand and raising her face to mine.

"And I'll kill whoever has struck such fear in you, whoever put those scars all over your body and marred your beautiful skin. Because no one causes such harm for anything *good*, and the sooner you realize that you have every right to fight back, the more powerful you'll become, *mia fiamma*."

Leaning down, I crush my lips to hers, tasting the sweetness of her lips as they move against mine. A small moan escapes her, and I grip her thighs to lift her onto the desk, keeping her body firmly pressed to mine as I devour her. My mouth moves from her lips to her cheek, trailing kisses over her jaw and down her neck to her collarbone. Her fingers bury into my hair, pulling me closer.

"It's as if the gods created you for me," I murmur. "Your lips were shaped to fit mine, and your skin was made to be touched by my fingers." I kiss her lips again, licking the seam between them. "You were made to be mine," I whisper against her lips. "Say it."

She moves to kiss me, but I pull back a fraction, staring into her eyes.

"Say it."

She glances down at my lips. "I... I..." Her gaze travels back up to my eyes, and she hesitates. "I can't." She pushes me back and jumps down from the desk, pressing her fingers to her lips as she moves toward the door.

I reach for her hand, wrapping my fingers around hers. "Adara?"

Pulling from my grasp, she rushes toward the door. "I have to go. I shouldn't be here. Th-this is wrong."

Her words feel like knives to my heart. "Wrong? How is this wrong?" I use my speed to get to the door first, blocking her path as she reaches for the door's handle.

Keeping her eyes trained down, she avoids my gaze. "I'm a witch. I shouldn't be here."

Narrowing my eyes at her, I put a finger under her chin and raise her gaze to mine. "You're also a wolf. You're part of my pack. You have every right to be here."

She steps back, shrugging off my touch again. "I'm a witch first, Gideon. I have people counting on me."

I scoff. "Counting on you for what? To be the one to take the punches? To be the canvas for their cruelty?" I reach out and grab her wrist, pushing up her sleeve to show the scars marring her skin.

She rips her arm from my hand. "You know nothing about my life."

"Because you never answer any of my questions," I growl. "I'm trying to protect you, to help you. How do you expect me to do that when you give me no information?"

She throws her hands in the air. "I never asked for your protection or your help!"

"So, I'm just supposed to let you die at their hands? Do you know what it means to be mated, little witch?" Crossing my arms over my chest, I step back and lean against the door, waiting for her to make eye contact before I continue. "It means if you die, half of my soul dies too."

She blinks a few times, chewing on her lower lip, and it takes everything in me to not cross the few feet between us and brush my thumb across that lip. After a moment, she shakes her head. "I don't care. I-I need to leave."

Running a hand through my hair, I move aside and let her walk through the door. I follow her through the bar and outside. "You can't lie to me. I can smell it on you—the lies, the fear, your attraction to me. Stop hiding who you are. Gods damn it all, just stay here and let me help you."

She whirls around, tears forming in her eyes. "You can't save everyone, so stop trying to force me into something I never wanted in the first place. I won't be your prisoner in a pack that obviously hates me just because you can't stand not being able to save everyone."

What did you do, you fool? You pushed her too far, my wolf snarls.

I suck in a breath as she walks away, stomping through the woods. Her raven flies down from the branches, landing on her shoulder and glancing at me as they disappear into the darkness of the forest. If I didn't know any better, I'd say he looked almost... sad. But that can't be right. Why would a witch's familiar be sad to see her leaving my bar?

Sighing, I try to shove my wolf back inside me, his growling and frustration echoing my own confused emotions over everything that's happened in the last few hours, and head back into the bar.

CHAPTER NINETEEN
Adara

SWIPING TEARS FROM MY CHEEKS WITH THE heels of my hands, I walk through the forest in the direction of my house. Kaylus's claws dig into my shoulder with each step.

"Addy... what're you doing?"

"Don't, Kaylus. I have to go home," I say, my voice shaking. "Jules is there alone, and Monique will be back in the morning, and I-I..." A sob escapes me, and I cover my mouth with one hand, the other pressing against my stomach.

"You know Jules will be fine. You're walking away from your destiny."

"How can you say that? He's a-a monster, and the coven is my f-family."

He nuzzles his beak into my cheek, ruffling his feathers. *"Because Gideon has done more for you in a short time than Monique ever has. You're actually happy when you're here, somewhere you're allowed to be yourself."*

Another sob breaks from my mouth, and I stumble over loose rocks, falling to my knees and bawling as my heart feels like it's being torn in half. My wolf is begging me to go back to him, but I can't abandon Jules and the life we want to build.

After a few moments, I gather myself up and trek the rest of the way home, the sun peeking through the bare trees. Noting that Monique's car isn't in the driveway, I slowly turn the front door's knob and slip inside. It's dark, all the curtains pulled shut, and I tiptoe toward the stairs. As I reach the bottom step, the living room light flicks on.

I yelp, jumping and putting a hand to my chest, my heart beating wildly.

"Where have you been?" Monique asks, sitting on the couch with her legs crossed. Her face is twisted into a look of disgust.

"Mom? I didn't know you were home." I take some deep breaths to calm my heart.

"Don't ignore me, Adara. Where have you been?" She clips each word, her expression darkening.

My throat tightens. "I... I, uh, was cleaning the yard."

"You weren't in the yard when I got home." She crosses her arm across her chest and purses her lips.

"I-I went for a walk after I finished." I consciously avoid wiping my sweaty palms on my leggings to hide my nervousness.

"So, you left Juliana here alone to go for a walk. And where did you walk to?" She stands up, grabbing a duffel bag from behind the couch and throwing it on to the dining table. "Was it to get this?"

The cash I've been saving up for Jules's tuition spills across the table and falls to the floor. Panic constricts my chest, making my lungs burn.

"Well?" Monique stalks toward me, pointing one hand at the cash on the table. Her heels clack on the floor, and she steps close enough for me to smell dark magic on her—like a faint whiff of sage and ashes. "You've been acting strange for a while now, and I knew you were up to something," she says quietly, fisting my shirt in her hand and yanking me onto the tips of my toes.

Monique isn't much taller than me—until she puts on her heels—and right now, she must have on stilettos to be towering over me like this. I try to swallow past the lump in my throat but the collar of my shirt is too tight. My fingers curl around her wrist, trying to pry her off and loosen her hold to get a breath of air.

"You smell just like them. Filthy mongrels." She releases me and throws me to the ground.

I lay there gasping for air, gulping in each breath between coughs as her words sink in slowly. "W-what did you say?" I ask quietly.

"You're a werewolf," she spits out.

"N-no. I-I'm not. I'm—"

Reaching down, she pulls me to my feet and slams me back into the wall, knocking the wind from my lungs. "Don't lie to me, Adara! I know exactly what you are. I can smell it all over you."

"Mama, stop, please!" My vision blurs, and the world spins around me as my head cracks the plaster when she slams me back again.

"Tell me the truth! Where did the money come from? Are you selling yourself to some pack bastard?" She screams in my face, rage dancing in her eyes.

"No," I whine. "I'm not. I'm just w-working, I swear."

She laughs bitterly in my face. "Like you could ever get a real job, Adara. Being a wolf's whore doesn't count as working."

"I'm not his whore." Gideon's face flashes in my mind, and my wolf whines, eager to be released and get us away from here. The mate bond burns in my chest, and I realize he was right. He never lied once when telling me about his family, their deaths... and he's never done anything but be exactly who he is. He's never worn a mask. He's never belittled me or made me feel worthless. He's the only one who's encouraged me to be stronger, and right now, I want nothing more than to be stronger—to fight back. But I can't leave Jules behind with this woman—this monster. "He was right about you—about all of this. You're just a bunch of murderers!"

Her hand cracks across my face, and I fall to the ground, cradling my burning cheek in one hand as tears slip down my face. "You're a traitor, a powerless witch, and the most worthless daughter I could ever have been cursed with." She crouches down, leaning over me as I curl into the fetal position on the floor. "Tell me everything you know about the pack you've joined, Adara, and maybe I'll let you live."

"I hate you," I bawl.

Grasping my chin in her hand, her nails dig into my cheeks as she turns my face to hers. "You will tell me everything." Her eyes burn holes into mine, and she mutters a charm under her breath. I try to struggle out of her grip, but her hand tightens its hold, blood dripping from the cuts in my face. "Who is your alpha?" she asks, her voice dangerously calm.

"G-G-Gideon Disantollo." The words are ripped from my throat despite every attempt to swallow them. My eyes go wide at the truth spell's power, and my wolf whines inside me.

"Is he the one who paid you?"

"Y-y-yes."

A small smile plays on her lips. "Did you have sex with him?"

"No," I answer, letting the answer out with as much venom as possible.

Her lip curls up. "Did you want to?"

"Y-yes." I gulp at the realization that if we had continued kissing in the lake, or in the office, I would've slept with him.

"Tell me about their pack. How do I capture one?"

"I don't know." I close my eyes in relief. Is this why Gideon never wanted me around the pack?

"What does that mean? You have to know something, Adara." Frustrated, her grip strengthens, cutting deeper into my cheeks.

I wince at the pain, blood dripping onto my chest. "I don't know how to capture one, I swear!"

"Fine." She stands, pushing my head down as she releases me, and I lay on the floor as the spell releases, panting and drenched in sweat. "If you won't choose your family over those mutts, then you'll die protecting them."

My eyes snap up to her as she reaches down to grab a fistful of my hair. "No, no, please!" Dragging me to the office door, she nudges it open with her foot and pulls me inside. She uses her heel to knock a book off one of the lower shelves, and it slides open to reveal a passage. Pulling me inside, the bookcase slides back in place, and darkness descends around us. I stumble after her as she pulls me along the hall, down the ramp, and into a musty basement I didn't even know existed.

Muttering a spell under her breath, she shoves me forward and ropes wrap around my wrists and ankles, binding me and keeping me close to the cold cement wall. "Don't worry, Jules is still fast asleep, but you will cooperate, or I can't guarantee her safety." A malicious smile splits her face as she pats my cheek gently. "Rest well, Adara."

I scream as she walks away, pulling against the binding ropes with all my strength, over and over. But it's useless. Her magic outweighs mine a thousand to one. Exhausted, I slump against the wall, unable to sit down with the short leads I've been given. Tears pour down my face, stinging the cuts on each cheek as the saltwater hits them. If I didn't know it before, I know it now, and as the truth settles deep into my mind and burrows its markings into my soul, my heart shatters—my mother has never loved me. Honestly, I don't think Monique is capable of loving anyone but her perfect self.

"Come on, come on," I murmur, trying to pull my wolf forward. My wrists tingle with each attempt, and my wolf whines, but she sounds distant, as if she were underwater.

Monique's lingering threat against Jules weighs heavily on me, and the more I struggle against the bindings, the more hopeless I feel. I have no powers to protect myself, nothing to protect Jules, and now Gideon and his entire pack are at risk because I couldn't fight off one witch. I hang my head, my arms pulled taut over my head, and cry as the helplessness consumes me. Eventually, exhaustion wins, and I fall into a restless sleep.

CHAPTER TWENTY
Gideon

I SIT AT THE BAR, LISTENING TO THE NEW shifter, Lucas, and his band play another classic rock cover song. The crowd has picked back up now that the live music is back, but I can't bring myself to care. I scan the bar again, noting that there's no raven-haired witch here yet tonight. I can't decide what's more annoying—waiting for her to show up and knowing she won't be coming back or knowing how much that thought makes my heart sink because I *want* her to show up.

My wolf cackles, mocking my thoughts. *I told you to chase after her, but as always, you fucked it up again.*

Growling, I snatch the whiskey glass off the bar after Frank sets it down and drain it in a few gulps.

"No Adara tonight, boss?" Frank asks, glancing up at me while wiping down the bar.

It's already nearing midnight, and there's been no sign of her. Ignoring him, I stare down into the empty glass, replaying last night in my head. The intimacy in my office, the fire in her temper, how alive she made me feel—whole after sharing my pain with her.

How stupid I was to brag about killing those witches, though I was honest. I'd do it again, and I plan to kill whoever gave her those scars, whether she's with me or not.

My wolf growls in agreement because no one touches our mate and lives to talk about it.

If you would've accepted her as your mate to begin with, we wouldn't be in this mess, my wolf snarls.

I push my glass across the bar to Frank, who refills it and places it back in front of me.

"You okay, Dee?" Aramin slides next to me along the bar, leaning her body against my shoulder as her chest presses into my side. She tilts her head to rest it against mine, and I shrug her off me.

"I'm fine, get back to work." I toss back my drink and stand.

Anger flashes across Aramin's face. "Are you still hung up on that stupid witch?"

Ice snakes down my spine, and my claws immediately lengthen as I whirl toward her and grab her throat. "What was that?"

Her eyes go wide as I lift her off her feet, my hand tight around her neck. "I-I..." she squeaks.

"Gideon," Frank warns, and I loosen my grip slightly with a snarl.

"Answer me," I demand, my voice barely above a whisper and filled with alpha influence. "I don't have time for your games, Aramin."

"I-I don't know what you see in her. She's just some stupid w-witch." Squeezing her eyes shut, her hands claw at my fingers, trying to pry herself free.

"What did you say to Rathmann? How does he know?" I yell, spit flying onto her face.

She tries to shrink back away from me. "I told him she was a witch." Crying, she starts to whimper. "I told him every time she showed up here so he could follow her back to her c-coven."

Dragging her to the door, I yank it open and throw her outside.

She falls to the pavement and looks up at me. "I was trying to help you, Dee! The council would kill you if they knew the truth like I do!"

"You were helping yourself and putting yourself in my business. Don't act like you care about anything but power, Aramin, it's pathetic."

"She was going to get us all killed, and you're too soft for your mate to see the truth," she says, venom lacing her words.

"Get away from here before I kill you myself," I growl, my anger overtaking my control as my wolf comes out. Fur splits through my skin as my clothes shred, the torn fabric falling to the ground around me, and my bones snap and break, reshaping into my four-legged form.

Aramin screams as I lunge at her, pinning her to the ground with my front paws on her chest, my jowls dripping onto her cheek. *"You're banned from this pack. If I so much as smell you, if I find out she's dead because of you, I'll hunt you down and kill you myself."*

Stepping back off her, I watch as she climbs to her feet and takes off into the woods, sobbing loudly as she runs away.

I turn back to the bar once she's out of sight and catch Frank's eye. He nods, whistling loudly to clear the bar and pulling out his phone, texting the hunters.

Pacing in front of the bar, I look over the ten wolves gathered before me. I throw the pillow Adara rested her head on yesterday to the ground before them. *"Sniff it, catch her scent, and find her. Find. Her."*

Each wolf sniffs the pillow before taking off into the woods, but as I learned last time, her scent pulls in various directions. Frank stands beside me, bowing his head low to the ground. *"They're all going in a different direction."*

"I know."

"They might not find her if her scent is charmed," he says slowly, looking at me from where he still has his head bowed low.

My lips curl back in a snarl. *"They have to."*

Frank stands beside me, waiting in silence. The hours pass with no one able to find a scent that allows them to track her. They overlap in circles around the bar, swirling around us like a mist. Frustrated, I move toward the forest.

"Gideon, you should wait here. If the hunters can't find her, there's magic at play. Witches could be casing the woods."

"I don't care, Frank. I'm finding her."

"It's true, isn't it? What Aramin said about her being your mate?"

I stop as my paws reach the shadows of the tree line, looking up at the sky filled with stars that remind me of Adara's eyes. *"I won't survive if something happens to her,"* I say softly. Glancing over my shoulder, I watch Frank nod, then take off into the woods. He howls as I leave, tracking her scent myself, trying to use the mate bond between us to find her.

I dig deep inside myself, searching for that cord that snapped taut between us at the lake when our kiss sealed the bond between us. Finding the tie between our souls, I focus intently on it and try to follow where it leads, like fate's thread to my destiny, but it constantly changes direction. Sharp turns through the forest bring me back to the lake, and I collapse on the grass, exhausted and frustrated, watching as the sun rises higher in the sky.

I slowly trace my way back to the bar, finding a small brown wolf sitting outside the doors.

"*Jaz, why aren't you in school?*" I pad over to her, sitting beside her.

"*Your mate is missing. It's all the pack can talk about. I'm here to help!*" She jumps up onto her feet, her tongue lolling out the side.

Chuckling, I nudge her shoulder with my paw. "*No, you need to go to school.*"

Her face falls. "*But I want to help.*"

My mouth feels dry, and I heave a deep breath. "*There isn't anything to do. I can't find her. She's untrackable.*"

Jaz tilts her head to the side, every bit the puppy. "*So, you're going to just give up? That's pretty pathetic.*"

Shocked, I look down at her, and she shrugs.

"*Don't get mad. You know it's true.*"

Laughing, I shake my head. "*No, I won't give up,*" I say, and her ears perk up. "*But you're still going to school.*"

Scowling, her ears flatten. "*Fine.*"

I shift back and head into the bar, throwing on some clothes and calling Frank. "Meet me here in fifteen minutes. I want the raven tracked instead, and if that doesn't work, no one sleeps until she's found."

"You got it, boss. I'll call the hunters back in."

CHAPTER TWENTY-ONE
Adara

A BUCKET OF ICE WATER DRENCHES ME FROM head to toe, and I wake up with a gasp, my entire body shaking from the cold.

"Wake up," Monique says. "We have much to discuss."

My teeth chatter, and I move to wrap my arms around my waist when the ropes pull taut, reminding me of where I am. "I-I-I don't k-know anyth-thing."

She laughs. "Oh, please. I just heard Batya's newest prophecy. Do you want to know what it was?"

I stare at the floor by her feet, and she moves toward me, grabbing my hair and lifting my face to hers.

"It was about you, of course. Traitorous bitten witch that you are." Her green eyes seem sharper, feeling like knives in my brain. "'One with nothing will reign above, bite with silver, markings and well. One with nothing with rise again, from the ashes like a phoenix, fire and flame.'"

"I d-don't even know what that means," I say.

"Don't play stupid, Adara. It's about you. Bitten by the Silver Wolf Pack. You're nothing with no powers. Is that why you let him bite you? Did you really think becoming a wolf would make you powerful?" She laughs again, a hand over her stomach.

"I didn't choose to be a wolf," I say, my anger rising. "I was doing it for Jules because someone has to show her what it means to be loved."

She wipes a tear from her eye as her laughter dies. "And what? They just bit you while you were out for a stroll being the best sister you could be?"

"No, they bit me because I was cheating them out of money to save enough for Jules' academy tuition. I just wanted to get her out of this house and away from your evil, miserable soul!"

Her hand whips out and slaps me across the face. "You shut your filthy mouth. You dare to talk to me with such disrespect when I've given you girls everything? What has that pack ever done for you, huh? Buy you food? Give you a roof over your head? You owe me for everything I've done for you!"

"I don't owe you for your own choice to have children." I spit out blood onto the ground, glaring at her. "Grandma was the one who cared for us until she died. It was her bedtime stories about Lockwood's well that gave me hope for getting rid of my wolf when I knew I couldn't count on you for any help."

"What well?" she asks, striding forward to grab my chin.

"The wishing well..." I say, uncertain.

She rolls her eyes. "Of course she told you those asinine stories about that stupid well."

"They weren't asinine. They're true. There's even someone guarding the well with dark magic. But you wouldn't know that because you never cared to be an actual parent and talk to us."

She raises her hand again, murmuring under her breath, and I brace myself for another slap. But then her fingers curl in, and a punch like brick lands on my collarbone. I scream, curling into myself as pain erupts down my chest and shoulder. The bone fractures, and my vision starts to fade to black. "You remember this the next time you open your mouth with that kind of disrespect for the only parent that's stuck around for you," she says, her voice low in my ear.

The fire in my chest and shoulder pulls me in and out of consciousness, and I lose track of time. The lack of windows in this hidden basement makes it impossible to know if it's been days or hours since I was taken down here, but the dryness in my mouth is a constant reminder that it's been a while. I keep trying to pull my wolf to the surface, but it's like she's trapped inside a bubble, unable to come out.

The stairs creak, and I suppress a groan when I hear footsteps. Leaving my head hanging down, I can only hope that she'll think I'm asleep and give up questioning me for now. Though, that didn't matter much last time with her ice water.

"Addy?" a voice whispers.

I look up, moaning in pain with the quick movement.

"Oh my gods, what did she do?" Jules rushes down the steps and begins to undo the rope.

"No, no, you have to leave."

Her brows furrow over her bright green eyes, glistening with tears. "I won't leave you like this. I used a tracking spell to find you. I knew she was lying... Let me get you out of here."

"You have to go, Jules. If she knows you helped me at all, she'll hurt you too. Please. I'll be fine, I promise." I take a deep breath, trying to think through the pain. "Go upstairs, take the money from the duffel bag behind the couch, and go find the raven outside. Tell him everything. He'll help you."

Tears fall down her cheeks. "I can't leave you like this, Addy. I-I..."

"You have to. Get out of here!" My vision blurs as I start to cry with her.

"I can take you with me—"

"No, she can't know that you helped me. Go!"

A door clicks shut upstairs, and we both jump, knowing she came back home.

"Go, Jules. Get out of here!"

"I won't leave until you're safe." She backs up to the stairs, casting a fire spell and pointing her fingers at the rope before rushing up into the house.

I watch the spark hit the rope and begin the fizzle at the strands. Hope swells within me, despite knowing that fire spells are an ancient magic no witch has been able to use in a millennium. The flames start to flicker, then peter out. Tears prick at my eyes, and I realize how utterly useless I am. I have a wolf I can't shift into and not enough magic to cast even a simple spell. A thud comes from upstairs, and a crash sounds soon after.

Dread coils in my gut. "Jules? Jules! Juliana!" I scream her name over and over, but no one comes downstairs for what feels like hours.

Eventually, Monique casually walks down the stairs, smiling from ear to ear. "How are you, Adara? Feeling better this evening?"

"What did you do to her? Where is Jules?" I pull against the ropes, screaming in agony when it pulls against my shoulder, moving my collarbone.

Monique laughs. "You stupid fool. You don't get to ask me questions. You're only alive so I can steal that immortality from your very soul."

"I won't let you. This world deserves better than to deal with you for the rest of existence." I clench my jaw, bracing for whatever blow will come next, but instead, she smiles.

"That's fine then. I do need your permission to successfully take the immortality essence from you. I guess we'll just see what it takes." She taps a finger to her chin, mocking me as she pretends to think. "Perhaps Juliana's life or the life of each member of your entire pack. Oh, I know," she snaps her fingers, "maybe Gideon Disantollo's head on a silver stake."

Jules's warm smile, singing and laughing as she sweeps and helps me clean, flashes in my mind. The memory of being wrapped in Gideon's embrace in the lake, his body pressed to mine before his lips crash down over me. The look in his eyes when he tells me about his wife and child and the witches who killed them. Frank and Mila at the bar, the love in their eyes and how nice they've always been to me.

Pure hatred burns in my chest, and my entire body feels as if it's burning from the inside out. Flames engulf me, starting at my fingertips and searing the ropes where they hold me in place. The fire grows, spreading over my body, yet I feel no pain.

Burn her alive, a voice—my wolf—snarls in my head.

"My thoughts exactly," I whisper, as the ropes turn to ash and release me.

Monique backs away toward the stairs, staring at me with wide eyes. "That's impossible. You have no magic. You haven't had any magic your whole life!"

"What's the matter, Mother? Are you afraid?" I hold my arms out to the sides, blasting flames from my palms. The flow of magical power pumping through my body feels like the highest high I've ever had.

"I'll never fear you," Monique says, backing up the stairs as I light the house ablaze from the basement up, laughing maniacally.

"I'll never let you hurt them! Do you hear me?" I scream, lighting the upstairs in flames when I notice Jules is gone. I can only hope she made it to Chloe's.

I make it outside to see Monique climbing into her SUV, hitting the gas pedal and peeling down the drive. I stand before the house, the inferno blazing behind me as the wood beams crack and collapse. My fire goes out as her car disappears from view, and I hope she'll never find Jules again. I collapse to the ground, unable to keep myself standing as the magic and adrenaline wear off, but as darkness threatens to pull me under, my wolf claws at my chest. I release control to her, relieved by the knowledge that she knows exactly where we need to go.

CHAPTER TWENTY-TWO
Gideon

SITTING IN MY OFFICE, I CONSTANTLY CHECK MY phone, my window open to allow for any of the pack's howls to alert me. I pace back and forth along the bookcases, struggling with sitting here and doing nothing. Dusk blankets the forest, then night falls soon after. The autumn breeze rustles the leaves outside, blowing the cold air through the window. I swear it carries Adara's scent, but I know better than to trust it. It's happened to me countless times before—thinking I can smell her, just to rush outside to the empty lot. My wolf whines anxiously, the bond weakening in our chest as it's been doing since she left.

Thunder claps overhead, and lightning flashes. Rain pours down, the smell of wet tar and decaying leaves filling the air along with the sound of rain pelting against the metal roof. I collapse into my chair, staring at the ceiling. What is happening to weaken the bond?

You know the answer, my wolf says.

Clenching my fists, I glare at the space above me. I hate that he's right—I do know the answer.

Adara's hurt. Whatever hell she's in is stripping away her life, or her wolf, and I'm going to kill whoever's responsible for her pain. I'll burn every coven alive just to find them and bring them the pain they deserve.

A knock sounds at the bar door, meek and quiet, and I almost dismiss it until it comes again more urgently. I walk out and pull the door open, brows raised at the sight of the black haired woman who's occupied my thoughts for hours—days—weeks, even. Relief pours through me at the sight of her standing on my doorstep. But my gaze travels down to the blanket she's wrapped in—one from my truck.

"I..." She licks her lips and swallows, my eyes darting to her mouth before traveling back up to her eyes. "I didn't know where else to go," she whispers.

Rain pelts the ground behind her, dripping from her hair into her eyes, and I reach out instinctively, grabbing her wrist to pull her inside and closing the door behind her. Her lips tremble, whether from the cold or something else, I'm not sure, but her scent quickly fills the small space between us. And it's fucking heavenly.

Planting my hands against the door on either side of her, I lean closer, her violet eyes widening slightly, but as her tongue darts out to lick her lips again, all other thoughts are gone.

I press my lips to hers, softly at first, but as a breathy moan escapes her lips, the pressure and intensity increase to almost painful. Almost. Her hand reaches up, curling into my hair and crushing me closer against her, and I inhale sharply, feeling the connection with my wolf grow stronger than it's been in years—decades. A metallic, tangy, almost sweet smell assaults me, and my control slips through my fingers.

Blood.

I break the kiss, pulling away sharply as I feel my fingers lengthen into claws that carve into the door beside her head. She shrinks back slightly, sucking her lower lip between her teeth in a way that has me suppressing a groan, but it's then that I notice the marks covering her face and neck in the light of the bar. Cuts and bruises cover her skin, slipping beneath the edge of the blanket. Her collarbone is swollen and red.

"What happened?" I growl, trying desperately to hold on to my wolf. My skin burns with the fur fighting to break free beneath its surface, and I know my eyes are silver.

Her eyes lower, and my anger flares at the submissiveness. Adara is strong, fierce, anything but submissive.

"Please don't make me ask again, *mia fiamma*."

Her gaze flicks to mine, and the hurt flashing in her eyes steals my breath. "My mother. She..." Her voice breaks, and she swallows thickly, closing her eyes as a tear runs down her cheek. "She tried to imprison me for eternity. She wants to kill my wolf. I-I set a fire to escape..."

My jaw clenches so hard my teeth ache, my fangs lengthening and piercing into my lower lip. "Where is she?"

"S-she's gone, but you can't do anything, or she'll hurt my sister. Sh-she'll hurt *you*." Her hand wraps around my forearm. "Please, Gideon. I-I just need some time to figure everything out. I can send Jules to the academy if I can make some more money. She'll be safe there. I—"

I brush my thumb along her lips. "You're not alone, little witch."

Fresh tears pour from her eyes, and she nods, her hands burying into my shirt.

"I can send my hunters to find your sister and make sure she's safe, but I told you, darling, I'm no hero. I'm every bit the monster you've always thought I am." I brush a strand of hair behind her ear, looking at her lips as her tongue darts out to lick them. "I'm the villain, and I'll burn the whole world down, sacrifice every innocent life in this world, just to save your soul." I wrap her in my arms and cradle her shaking body to mine, pressing my lips to her hair. "Tomorrow, we'll deal with this, but for now, let's get you cleaned up. Let me take you home."

Thank you so much for reading Adara and Gideon's story. Please consider leaving a review on Goodreads or Amazon. Every review helps bring more visibility for new books. Keep reading for a name guide and the blurb for book two, LYCAN WITCH, coming fall of 2023!

NAMES: PRONUNCIATIONS AND WHAT THEY MEAN

Adara Morrow: a-dah-rah moor-oh – flames of tomorrow
Juliana: joo-lee-ah-nuh – youthful
Monique: moh-neek – alone

Gideon Disantollo: gid-ee-uhn dee-san-toh-loh – great destroyer, Hades
Ella: el-luh – fairy maiden
Grace: gr-ay-s – blessing

Frank: fr-ay-nk – free man
Mila: mee-luh – friendly
Aramin: ar-ah-min – mint (based on Minthe)
Darrold: dar-oh-ld – pride and honor
Kurtis: kur-tiss – refined
Lucas: loo-cas – bringer of light
Cali: cah-lee – lovely

Allen Rathmann: ah-len rah-th-man – great counselor

Madrona: mah-dr-oh-nuh – mother goddess
Jazelle: jah-zeh-l – pledge
Bella: bell-luh – beautiful

Wendell: wen-del – wanderer

Anera: ah-neh-ra – sand

Keith: kee-th – woods
Aaron Kilch: ayr-ren k-ill-ch – strong fish (codfish – *Peter Pan* inspired)

Chloe: k-loh-ee – servant of Demeter
Batya: bah-tee-yuh – heavenly
Celeste: sell-leh-st – daughter of god

Sawyer: soy-yer - woodcutter
Tristan: trih-st-an - sad

THE STORY CONTINUES...

Don't miss the breathtaking sequel, LYCAN WITCH, coming this fall 2023!

One kiss completes the bond—the alpha's mate hunted as a lycan witch.

Everyone knows not to cross Gideon Disantollo, the dangerous alpha of the Silver Wolf Pack, and every witch knows not to enter his territory... But gambling in his bar lands me bitten and changed, and I quickly realize Gideon is the only one I can turn to.

Because I never expected to be hunted by both sides—my coven and the lycan council. And I definitely didn't expect my mother to lead the hunt.

Now, I'm desperately trying to control the growing powers within me—the witch's ancient fire and my wolf, who grows stronger with each day spent near our mate—as I hunt for the dark witch guarding the Lockwood Forest wishing well.

And I have to do something about this mate bond between me and Gideon… before it's too late for us both.

Find it on Amazon here!

Story updates, ARC reader opportunities, and fun freebie extras available when joining the monthly newsletter! Visit www.whitneymorsillo.com to join.

ABOUT THE AUTHOR

Whitney Morsillo is a New England transplant living in the Tennessee mountains and writes YA paranormal romance. She has a master's in creative writing and believes books are crucial to survival in this wild world because "whether life is good or shit-tastic, you deserve an escape to beautiful men and to run with the wind in your fur... or hair." When she isn't writing swoon worthy, morally grey men who find their sassy fated mates to be their greatest strength—and infuriating weakness—or beautiful villains with tragic pasts, she looks forward to the changing leaves of autumn, drinks way too much Earl Grey tea, and reads her children *Harry Potter* while sneaking in some steamy reads after bedtime.

Follow her on Facebook, Instagram, TikTok, and Amazon!

Made in United States
North Haven, CT
22 May 2023